P9-CEU-260

LAND OF
BARBED
BOUNDARIES

**Center Point
Large Print**

**This Large Print Book carries the
Seal of Approval of N.A.V.H.**

LAND OF BARBED BOUNDARIES

Lauran Paine

Center Point Publishing
Thorndike, Maine

This Center Point Large Print edition
is published in the year 2005 by arrangement with
Golden West Literary Agency.

Copyright © 2005 by Mona Paine in the U.S.
Originally published in Great Britain
by Robert Hale & Co. © 1975.

The text of this Large Print edition is unabridged. In other
aspects, this book may vary from the original edition. Printed in
Thailand. Set in 16-point Times New Roman type.

ISBN 1-58547-580-7

Library of Congress Cataloging-in-Publication Data

Paine, Lauran.
     Land of barbed boundaries / Lauran Paine.--Center Point large print ed.
        p. cm.
     ISBN 1-58547-580-7 (lib. bdg. : alk. paper)
     1. Large type books. I. Title.

PS3566.A34L36 2005
813'.54--dc22

                                                                    2004025055

Chapter One

A LONE RIDER

Dave reined up near the juniper and swung down. It was pre-dusk on a hot summer day and what prevailed was that long, dying fullness of warmth that becomes a sort of embryonic twilight.

He dangled the left rein from his gloved fist and dropped wearily to the ground in the pungent-scented shade. The horse moved in closer too, and relaxed. It was stifling hot.

Dave saw the cattle in rushes down by the creek, brushing irritably at the devilish heel-flies. The brockle-faced heifer was with them; the one old Lester had sent him out to look for—only now she wasn't a heifer any more. There was a calf beside her. Now she was a cow. Dave watched her with a small, tired sense of relief. He was a little disgusted, too. Six hours astraddle in the summer sunblast, riding, looking and sweating, and half-way back to the ranch he'd found her.

The humid warmth of the upland hill country was oppressive. Dave felt the sweat drift along the furrows of his forehead, gather above his nose, trickle down it and drop lazily to the parched earth. He made a cigarette and fished for a match. The effort made his spurs ring musically. The horse opened one eye, regarding him briefly, then lapsed back into somnolence. He lit and exhaled. The heavy atmosphere had two effects. One, it made his feet feel swollen and pulpy in their boots. And this other sensation, while not new either, was more intense than it had been before.

It had to do exclusively with Dave Reed, and yet there was a sea of other faces in the grey background, too. Other riders. Some he still knew, and others he had known. It was a sad, lonely feeling. All old riders knew it once in a while—and not just riders. It is the passing of time and the moment of reflection.

Dave watched the cows drift out of the rushes as the sun sank beyond a hill somewhere. He was in his middle thirties, still had his horses, his saddle, his craving to ride and drink and laugh, but now there was this uncomfortable realization, getting more insistent lately, that he was becoming an ageing rider.

The picture of other riders, even older, came up. It wasn't pleasant, what time was doing to them. Then there were the boys who no longer showed up at the saloons on Saturday night. Someway, there now existed a sort of barrier against them. They were rarely mentioned any more, and when they were, one could sense the nostalgia. And there were the new faces, too. The younger cowboys who kept coming on, that Dave and the others had nothing in common with.

There were the Craig Cramers, too. They had their own cattle and range, and were prospering. They didn't drink with old pardners any more, and hardly ever roped in the roundups. They sat with their families at the Fourth of July celebrations, in the new park at Danville under the scraggly sycamores, and laughed as little kids crawled over them.

Dave deftly raised a booted foot and rolled the cigarette to death, decapitating the fiery end and watching it die. He grunted to his feet and ran a finger under the cinch, shrugged and swung up. If anything, the earth seemed to expel more heat at the close of the day, after the sun was gone, than it had while the brilliant disc hung in the brassy sky.

He rode back to Bar Seven slouch-shouldered and solemn. The hollow feeling of being left behind, of chasing youth ahorseback, while others matured and acquired things, persisted. It was still there, inside of him and even reflected in his face, when he rode into the large, dusty yard of Bar Seven and dismounted by the corrals, unsaddled and turned his horse out.

He heard Lester coming out of the huge old barn and walking towards him. He knew it was Lester because the boots didn't ring with spurs. Dave also knew that Lester, with his stern single-mindedness, had a thinly disguised contempt for all cowboys and the irresponsibility they stood for. He didn't turn when Lester spoke. Just went right ahead hanging his saddle from the low limb in the sycamore, by one stirrup.

"Find her, Dave?"

"Sure." Dave felt irritability arising within him. He turned slowly. "That's what you sent me out for wasn't it?"

Lester's brown eyes regarded him levelly for a long second before he nodded his head. "Yas. Where was she?"

Dave knew what was coming then, too. That odd feeling of being static in a progressive world was leaden inside of him. He was dissatisfied with himself. It

7

showed in the way he regarded the big man who owned Bar Seven.

"Over by Clear Creek. On the way back from Mesa Meadows."

Lester blinked slowly. "About two hours' ride from here?"

Dave nodded. He knew there was no answer. "Yeah. About that far, I reckon."

"You were all day gettin' there, Dave?"

"No, not by a damned sight. If I'd known where she was, I'd have ridden there first. I figured she'd be with that bunch that stays with the Arrowhead bull, and I rode for the Meadows first. Didn't find her until I was on my way back."

"Oh." Lester Mallow had a way of saying things like that "Oh," that slathered listeners with half-scorn, sometimes. Dave Reed was in no mood to overlook innuendos. He spat lustily to relieve the scorch in his throat.

"Oh—what, Lester?"

The big, grizzled man was moving away. He stopped, turned his head without quite moving his body, and stared at Dave. There was that sheen of contempt showing in his dark, bright eyes. Scorn for everything Dave Reed stood for. Riders, their instability, their reck-lessness, savagery, shell-belts and guns, and even the wasted silver on their spurs, saddles and bits. Lester Mallow had never been a good rider—a good rancher, yes, but not a good cowboy. They stood looking at one another, worlds apart. Then Lester turned his thick body and pushed his hands into the levi pockets.

"Just what I said, Dave. Oh."

"You figure I took the whole day to find the heifer. Is that it?"

Lester struggled with his temper. A rich cowman, maybe a little impatient and exacting, he was, nevertheless, not an unfair man, and certainly not dishonest, with himself or others.

"Well—you were out close to eight hours. That cost me as much as the calf'd fetch."

The resentment swelled in the rider. Anger that sprang from nowhere—unless it was a form of envy for Mallow's endless sweep of land and great herds. Anyway, it was anger. It showed, too, and Lester braced against it, standing there, massive legs spread a little, and hands fisted in his pockets.

But Dave's voice was calm when he spoke. "Listen, Lester. You send a man out to do a job and he does it the best way he knows how. Costs be hanged. He can't do any better."

"No," Lester said slowly. "I expect not." Then he turned and stalked towards the house.

There it was again. Lester's way of saying something that didn't quite get to the listener until the man had gone. Dave made a cigarette, and smoked it, while full understanding soaked in.

In effect, Lester meant no rider was intelligent enough to understand costs. How the successful cowman operated. Riders were ignorant; too stupid to see the difference between being successful—and a cowboy.

What made it worse, too, was that Lester's reasoning fitted in exactly with what Dave's mood of dissatisfaction was telling him, with its small, inner voice.

Lester Mallow had got ahead. Forged an empire. Dave Reed was nothing, now, that he hadn't been ten years before. He spat in his gloved hand, snuffed out his cigarette, went into the barn and forked hay to the horses. While he was in there, choring, he heard the other Bar Seven riders swing down outside. Normally he would have gone out and joined in the eternal, barbed hazing that is the cowboy's forte, but that evening he didn't.

Bar Seven had eleven-thousand acres, deeded, and a turn-out right on the out-range for six-thousand head. It was big, even for cattle country. Lester Mallow ruled it from the big house. He rarely rode, preferring a buggy. No one said much about this in a land where every able-bodied man rode astride. The rich and powerful had privileges. Dave understood all this.

Six years as head rider for Bar Seven had shown Dave a lot of things about old Lester. How he became more preoccupied as his wealth and investments grew. Less tolerant of the riders' pranks, remote, in a sense, from everything that didn't immediately affect his empire and its accruing wealth. Dave wasn't a vindictive man, but lately his dissatisfaction and the glaring obvious aloofness of Lester had begun to build a deep and abiding irritability in him. And then there was the persistent, growing personal dissatisfaction, now, too.

There was something else, though, that kept him on the Bar Seven. Lester's daughter. Lucy Mallow was everything to Dave that her father wasn't. Handsome, in a full-bodied way, full of laughter, pretty as a wild

10

flower, and brimming with generous affection for Bar Seven's head rider, Dave Reed. And that, also, had grown slowly, almost unnoticed, until Dave Reed and Lucy Mallow had told each other. It was love, as natural and as poignant as it could be. And here, again, was another rub that formed and sustained the dissatisfaction. What could he offer Lucy? Nothing.

"Hello."

Dave started suddenly and turned. It was Mrs. Mallow, Lester's wife. Anne, everyone called her. She was still pretty. An earthy woman and shrewd, there was a sense of ruggedness to her. It was in her eyes, the cant of her jaw and the erect carriage. Lucy had got the sense of humor from her mother, although the years had taken the spontaneous edge off it, for Anne. Dave smiled. He was genuinely fond of Anne, like everyone else in the Mesa country. She studied his face in silence, then made some darting movements with her head.

"Looking for eggs, Dave. Some of those darned hens are stealing their nests out. You see any in the hayloft?"

It was a welcome, wholesome respite from the acid of his thoughts. He relaxed and hung the hay-fork on its two nails. "No, haven't seen a hen in there, Anne." He turned towards her. "I'll help you look, though."

"No." She straightened up again, almost as tall as he was. Something in her tone brought him around, looking at her. She wasn't smiling. He had a quick hunch she wasn't really looking for eggs at all, and turned full to face her.

"Dave—what did you and Lester argue about?"

He heard the riders talking as they turned their mounts

11

out and draped their saddles. "We didn't argue, Anne. Not really." Then he recited the conversation with Lester.

Anne nodded slowly. "That's all there was to it, Dave?"

"Yes'm." He had an uneasy premonition. "Why?"

"Well, Lester asked me to send you around to the office."

Dumbfounded, they stood there, unbelieving. In six years Dave had come to know that summons. A rider was going to be paid off. Fired.

The clump of boot-heels with the gay music of spur rowels was coming towards the barn. It interrupted their silence like a knell, which, in a way, it was, to Dave Reed's long association with the mighty Bar Seven outfit. His mouth had that peculiar slit of white over the upper lip that was always there when he was seething inside, then he bowed slightly.

"Thanks, Anne, I'll go around."

He was almost past her, and felt the look on her face rather than saw it. He stopped. "I'm sorry, Anne. Real sorry. Will you tell Lucy for me?"

She nodded. There was the wisdom of a long life in a rough land in every strong line of her face. Knowledge and understanding of hurt, too. "Yes, I'll tell her, Dave. But hadn't you better see her before you go? She's in the kitchen with Juanita." The hazel eyes wavered, went soft, then hardened again. If Anne wanted to say more, she didn't.

Lester was sitting behind his old desk when Dave entered the office. It had been built on to the back of the house and was the heart of the Bar Seven. Here Lester

12

Mallow ran his empire. Two chairs, a long bench nailed to one wall and some stockman's calendars hanging on the walls, were the unimaginative furnishings of the room. Lester was sitting at the desk. Dave wanted to get it over with. He faced Lester over the desk with a stony face.

"Got it made out, Lester?"

The big rancher didn't answer, just held the check and watched the rider stuff it into his shirt pocket. If he was going to speak, he never got the chance. Dave dumped the load off his mind in staccato sentences, then paused, looked down at the older man and shrugged. He felt the hopelessness of them ever meeting on common ground. Truly, they were worlds apart.

"Lester—you're a good rancher. Too good, maybe. I reckon I hadn't ought to say any more, but dammit, there's something like humanity that you're overlooking; I don't know exactly what it is, but it's there, anyway."

Lester looked up at Dave with no show of animosity, which puzzled the younger man. In fact, there was a sort of vaguely speculative, cynically wondering look in Mallow's features. He wagged his head back and forth evenly. "You're overlooking something, too, Dave. Growing up, I think. Well—all right, Dave. We'll both live through this. I wonder what's next—for you."

Dave was still interpreting the half-spoken thoughts when he nodded curtly and went out of the office door, striding towards the corrals. He was half-way there when he remembered Lucy. He still went to the corrals, though, caught his horses, saddled one and packed the other, tied them in the shade of the sycamore tree, smoked a parting cigarette in silence, and alone, before he went back through the gathering gloom towards the rear of the house, where the big dining-room was off the kitchen.

Lucy was standing outside in the fragrant shadows, like she had known he was coming to her. Which she had; Anne had told her. She watched his firm, solid approach and admired him for the thousandth time.

Dave heard the desultory, small racket of the dining-hall and noticed the unusually subdued atmosphere. He knew the Bar Seven riders were adjusting to the news of his dismissal.

"Lucy, honey."

"Anne told me, Dave." She leaned towards him a little. "It had to happen, someday, didn't it?"

He nodded. A wave of sadness engulfed him. "I reckon, Lucy."

The girl smiled wistfully. "I—just thought it would always be the same. You and me and Bar Seven. Kind of a part of each other. Together." She looked down at her hands. "That was sort of childish, wasn't it?"

Dave looked at her with a sense of discomfort and wonder. "You sound like I'm going to be buried, Lucy."

"Well—you'll be riding away, won't you?"

There it was. He knew then that Lucy thought like everyone else did. Cowboys were drifters. Fire one, and he saddled up with a laugh, relieved that he was no longer tied to a fealty, and drifted on into the sunset—irresponsibility on horseback.

In a flash he knew he didn't want this life any longer.

It was the age—the slow, reluctant maturity—that had crystallized inside of him, into a brutally honest picture of himself at the turning point of his life.

"Lucy—we've been kids. You are a kid. I'm ten years older. I should've known better." She was smiling uncertainly at him. "You know something, Lucy? Lester's right about some things. Maybe he's too right, like he's too good a rancher, but anyway, he's right." He took her hand and held it.

"No, I'm not going away. I'm going to stay on the Mesa, and you're going to wait for me, Lucy, until I'm ready, then you're going to marry me."

"Ready, Dave?"

He shook his head. "I haven't figured what that means yet, honey. But you wait."

"Yes," she said. "I'll wait, Dave."

He kissed her then, and didn't care whether Lester saw them this time or not. Lester didn't though. He was busy eating at the head of the table, watching his plate, as were the wooden-faced Bar Seven riders.

But Anne saw them. She hadn't been hungry anyway, so she stayed in the kitchen with Juanita, the Indian house-girl, and puttered at the drainboard by the window, and watched the fading light of the spent day—and her only daughter.

Chapter Two

MOVE ON

The usual sense of being footloose and on the move was lacking as Dave rode away from the Bar Seven towards Danville. Too many ties, indissoluble and hardening into bonds he scarcely understood, conflicted with the old, wild spirit. The night was balmy warm with a crescent torch in the tattered tapestry of the heavens. Dave rode drowsily over the sighing, parched range until the lights of Danville, small squares of orange lamp-light, showed ahead, then he swung above the town, cut the stage road and rode silently past three huge hulks of freight wagons, where a supper fire burned, and descended on the town.

Danville, as a town, was typical of the frontier, except that it had shade, and of late, a city-sponsored park that was still held in uncomfortable awe by the single riders from the surrounding ranches of the Mesa. Progress, staid and slightly stiff-necked, had come. With it, had come a civic sense rarely found on the frontier. The changing times brought other things, too. Like the scramble for land on speculation, and the violence of the big cow outfits against those who would confine them, and the freight loads of things new to the Mesa, like ploughs with garish, red painted frame-works, that leaned ominously against the checked paint and warped siding of the Danville Emporium.

But the riders still shrugged off these sinister omens

that were portents of the future, and gathered in Colton's Saloon to drink and argue and shout, and fight with the guns they wore, and laugh, too, while the big cowmen sat uneasily at their headquarters and watched the inevitable change of the Great Plains and prepared to resist, as they had the Indians, lawless invaders, and the savage elements themselves. Born and bred in a fighting land and era, matured in violence, the cowmen were facing another foe as they had all others. With guns!

Dave stabled his horses and wandered into Colton's Saloon. The aloneness left him when he swung through the louvered doors and smelled the close, hazy atmosphere. He had always admired the majestic, seven-point buck over the back-bar mirror, where its glassy eyes stared above the bedlam, keeping an eternal vigil on Eternity. Someone tapped his arm lightly. He looked around, saw the sweaty, red face of Jerry Turk, an Arrowhead rider, grinning at him.

"Jeezuz! Old Lester let you off? How come? Buy you a drink?"

Dave elbowed into the mob of men with a mechanical smile. Jerry clamored for service from a sallow bartender with a fierce moustache, who was sweating through his silk shirt. They had the drink, then Dave bought the next one. A big dark visaged man loomed up, jostled his way in close, eyed Dave familiarly and smiled. It was George Marsters—foreman of the Arrowhead, the big outfit adjoining Bar Seven. Hard as a rock, grim looking, a taciturn, brooding man whose massive body and black features were better than words at telling the story of his hardness.

"How come you in town, Dave?"

The noise of Colton's place was rasping and insistent, but Dave's one word carried well enough. The shock of surprise, more than the word itself, carried.

"Fired."

Jerry Turk's head jerked. He stared from one side, as George Marsters stared from the other. They were startled speechless. Bar Seven without Dave Reed was unimaginable. George thought of Lucy, started to say something with a wry twist of his mouth, thought it over and didn't say it. He looked down at the thick glass of ale.

Jerry Turk spoke in his high, crackling voice. "Well— I'll be goddammed!"

There was a gloom of silence hanging over the three men when someone clapped Dave lightly on the shoulder. He turned, saw deputy sheriff Dick Newton, smiling easily at him, and smiled back. Dave had always liked the deputy. Newton was tall, a very thin man whose movements were jerky, like the tendons that operated his joints had been dehydrated some way, sucked dry of their natural juices. As emaciated perhaps, as the long, alarmingly cadaverous body. Coarse featured, but the calm tolerance and shrewd appraisal that had made Abraham Lincoln ugly and handsome, at the same time, Dick Newton's face was not homely. The jerky, abrupt movements of his body apparently didn't extend to his hands and arms. Boot Hill attested that, as did his reputation.

"Buy you boys one?"

Jerry Turk gave way a little. Deputy Newton edged in. He didn't take up much space. The bartender shot them glances of inquiry. They all had rye whisky and Jerry nudged the deputy.

"Lester fired him."

Dick absorbed this stoically enough, but looked at Dave, in case the cowboy wanted to add anything. He didn't. They all drank, then George Marsters turned slowly, ponderously. His thick features were heavy and flinty. He wore a small sandy beard that added to the ominousness of his general appearance.

"Arrowhead'll hire you, Dave. Ride back with us. I'll put you on tomorrow, so's you won't lose a day. Pay you as much as Lester did, too."

Jerry nodded at Dave. "G'almighty yes. Hire out to him. Arrowhead's a good outfit. I been on for three years now."

Deputy Newton cocked an eye at George. "Well— that settles it. You keep Jerry that long, George, anybody could work for Arrowhead."

It was the customary hazing; the heavy humor that was as much a part of cowboys as the air they breathed. They all laughed, then Dave wagged his head at the bartender and had a repeat set up.

"No thanks, George. I got a little loafing coming. Got something on my mind, sort of. I'll maybe ride out the end of the week, if you'll still have the spot."

George's hawk-like profile didn't answer, but his head came up gradually with the shot-glass. He spoke before the liquor stung into his throat. "Sure, Dave; anytime." He nodded to the others and drifted back into the crowd.

A busty, stocky woman with a glassy look came up and rubbed against Jerry Turk. He smiled for once without laughing. It was a primitive smile with something cruel in it. He hooked her arm and was lost in the jostling mob of noisy riders, and only Dick Newton and Dave Reed were still leaning where they had been. The slight space vacated was quickly filled by more shouting, cursing riders.

Newton closed his bony fist over the shot-glass, then opened it suddenly. He repeated this movement idly for several seconds before he spoke. A sidelong glance showed him that Dave was lost in his own thoughts.

"Doing anything right now, Dave?"

"No. Thought I might get drunk tonight, though." He said it with a little dry laugh. "Why?"

"Well—whyn't you walk over to the office with me."

Dave studied the thin man's calm, emotionless face, shrugged and nodded. "Let's go. I'll get drunk later."

Outside, the air was fragrant with the rising odor of curing grass and drying manure in the wide roadway. They ducked around a loaded hitchrail and crossed through the dust, stepped up on to the plankwalk across the way and strolled past idlers out in the night's benevolent coolness, and went into the deputy's office where a far door hid three strap-iron cages, sitting side by side, which were the cells of Danville's jailhouse.

"Seat," said Newton, motioning towards a bench that covered the entire north wall of the little office. Dave sat, fished for his tobacco and watched Dick ease his frame into an amply padded, cane-bottomed chair.

They smoked in silence for a moment. The sounds

from Colton's Saloon were distinct but muted. Dick took a roping glove from his hip pocket and mopped the sweat off his bronzed forehead.

"Dave—county seat's sent me a letter asking for recommendations of another deputy to be stationed here in Danville, with me."

"Oh?"

"Yeah. When Jerry said you'd been fired off Bar Seven—well—I sort of thought this might fit you like a glove. An act of Providence, kind of."

Newton took off his hat and dropped it on to the messy table in front of him and ran a hand through the jungle of his sweaty hair. "You'd be the man I'd pick, if I was picking them." He shrugged. "Never thought of you, though. Always seemed like you'd die on the Bar Seven."

Dave made a short laugh. "Seems like I been there long enough, all right." Then he fell silent, still looking at the end of his cigarette. The feeling inside of him was still there, and for some crazy reason, it seemed pleased at the prospect of being a deputy sheriff. Still, he was unsure. Making changes had come harder, the last few years. Then he thought of Lucy, and the thing's he'd said to her. His imagination grasped this, and wove a yarn house with yard hollyhocks growing on it, at the edge of town. It would be security and steady pay, and much more than a top rider would make. Providence, Dick had said. He looked up, caught Newton's steady gaze on him and nodded a little.

"Might be at that, Dick."

"What?"

"Providence." Dick still regarded him levelly, saying nothing. "All right. What do I have to do?"

Newton swept his hat aside and leaned over the table with his jerky, quick movements, found the letter from the county seat, turned it over and deliberately wrote with a stubby pencil on the back. There were only two sounds in the hot little office. The racket that seeped in from the saloon, and the rustling of the paper under Newton's pencil. Dick didn't even read what he had written; just folded it and handed the paper to Dave.

"Ride over to Glenwood tomorrow and give that to Sheriff Stanley. If he's agreeable, he'll swear you in and send you back here. I'll break you in. Starting pay's ninety-dollars a month, and keep for one horse."

"Well," Dave felt uneasy. The clot of restlessness was making its last inner appeal, then he shrugged, thumbed back his hat and wagged his head ruefully. "Damn. Things sure happen fast, sometimes, don't they?"

Dick smiled. "Yeah. Seems that way. Anyway, between us, there's not much to this job any more. Sure, Stanley thinks there's going to be need for more help because the Mesa's growing to beat the devil, with these grangers and all. It's mostly drunk riders though. Once in a while a kill-happy Mexkin. Maybe a horse thief or two, or fighting teamsters. Not like it was two–three years ago. Mesa's changing a lot. Danville, too. Emigrants've sort of taken the guts out of the country, seems like. They're like sheep. Most of 'em don't even carry guns. Homesteaders!" He said the word like it was bile, and let it lie there, an epitome of

22

everything a born cowman like Dick Newton detested, then he smiled again.

"Used to be a fight every couple of days. Now it's some granger that's lost his team-horse—or something." He shrugged. "Not hardly any work for the money any more, Dave, but it's better pay than cowboying and a whale of a lot easier, too."

Infused with the uncertainty that goes with a new job, a new life, Dave pocketed the letter and stood up. He grinned, masking the doubt. "Come on, Dick, buy you a drink on this."

Newton got up abruptly and threw a tight smile back at Dave. "Now you got two things to get drunk over, huh?"

But it wasn't that way. Dave didn't get drunk after all. By the time he had traded drinks with Dick, the desire to forget himself was gone, and in its place was a new sensation of wanting to be alone for a while. To lie some place and think. He left the saloon, shuffled through the velvety night to the public corral where his horses were, made up a pallet and lay on it, clothed except for his hat, shell-belt and gun, and spurred boots, and looked up at the great, somber vault of Heaven.

The ride to Glenwood, county seat of the Mesa country, was made mostly during the pre-dawn and early light. It was the coolest part of the day. Of the entire summer, for that matter.

Dave stabled at a huge place swarming with horses and hostlers, felt a little lost and out of place in the bustle of the larger town, but doggedly went to the court house, found Sheriff Stanley and gave him Dick's letter.

There was a very solemn faced pendulum clock behind the Sheriff's desk that made a monotonous, deep, throbbing sound with each beat of its sluggish heart. Stanley was bald, pale, portly and gimlet-eyed with a formidable jaw. He smiled at Dave, appraised him in a flash and extended his hand. The swearing in was brief; issuing identification briefer, and suddenly Dave was back in the dingy corridor, with its oiled, dark floors, a deputy sheriff with a new badge and two letters to take back to Dick.

Still a little dazed, he ambled aimlessly back towards the stairway that led out of the court house, and was engulfed by a mob of people crowding into a huge room that smelled of sweat and onion sandwiches. Borne along, he didn't get clear of the press until he was face to face with a huge map with a lot of penciled squares on it. A young man with violet sleeve-garters glowered at him.

"Got your description?"

"What description?"

The man's exasperation and perspiration were merged. "Jeezus!" he said violently. "Don't any of you . . . !"

"Rope it, hombre!" Dave's rancor sprang up instantly to face the man's wrath. "I got shoved in here by this damned crowd."

The fire died out in the man's eyes. He saw the badge and eyed it studiously, then his raffish face lit suddenly with humor and he laughed in an abrupt, nasal voice. "Oh, hell, I thought you was one of—these." He waved a white hand at the sea of dull faces around them, crowding. "Homesteaders." He pronounced it the same way Newton did. With deep disgust and scorn. Someone, an old man, plucked timidly at the man's handsome sleeve-garter and spoke. Dave was jostled and eased back gently by the crowd. Someone stumbled over his spurs. Nettled, he elbowed his way out of the press and leaned against a far wall, disheveled and annoyed.

A little awed, too, by the strangeness of the scene, Dave watched. He had never seen people so intensely eager and hopeful as this crowd of strangers was. There wasn't a cowman or a rider among them. A lot of them didn't even speak English. His eyes wandered back to the map and read the bold, black legend across the top. LAND AVAILABLE UNDER THE HOMESTEAD ENACTMENT OF 1862. Letting his gaze roam over the huge panel that covered the entire west wall, he saw the Mesa country was included. Naturally, his eyes sought the familiar boundaries of the Bar Seven. And then he straightened. The grassy, tremendously bountiful Mesa Meadows country, where Bar Seven and Arrowhead ran their cattle first, for the early spring feed, was clearly outlined as public domain.

Dave stood motionless for a long time, looking over the crowd of shapeless hats, eyes on the big map. He was held firmly in the grip of a sudden, wild idea, and some of the ramifications that went with it. Homestead Mesa Meadows! A word of Dick Newton's rattled around inside his head. Providence. Mesa Meadows and Lucy. A ranch and a wife. He must have one in order to acquire the other.

Later, the man with the elegant violet sleeve-garters looked up and saw the very sober-faced deputy sheriff regarding him woodenly. He blinked his surprise. "You come back?"

Dave shook his head without looking away from the man's round face. "I never left." He raised a hand and pointed to the fine lines that indicated Mesa Meadows on the map. "You know how a man goes about home-steading that land up there?"

The shorter man craned his neck and scowled. "Hell," he said disgustedly. "That's way in back of Danville. No road or nothing in there. You don't want . . ."

"I know that land, Mister. How do you go about fixin' up the papers and all that?"

The office was almost empty. The clerk looked at him closely. "For five dollars and a twenty minute wait. I'll do it for you."

Dave gave the man five dollars and stood studying the map for what seemed like seconds with an awful sensa-tion in his stomach. He was frightened at what he was doing. If Bar Seven or Arrowhead knew—if Deputy Newton knew—in fact the way sentiment was, if anyone in the Mesa country knew or found what he had done, Dave Reed would be worse than a clod-hopper, because he, at least knew better.

"Here you are, Deputy." The man had it all in a thick envelope. "Rules are in there, too. Tells you what you got to do to prove up."

"Prove up?"

"Yeah." The raffish face bobbed irritably. "It's all in there. Do like it says and you got yourself a piece of land." The man looked at him steadily for a long moment, then spoke again. "You figure to make a cattle place up there?"

Dave considered this thoughtfully, then nodded. He didn't speak. The words were all damned up behind his teeth.

"I thought so." He tapped the envelope in Dave's hand. "Well, you only got a section in there. If you want two more sections, adjoining, I'll take care of 'em for you—map 'em and block 'em off the plat—for three cents an acre. Want 'em?"

Dave figured quickly and squinted at the man. "You got a stick?"

A pointer was produced and Dave showed the clerk exactly what was the best land in the meadows, then he handed the man back the pointer and figured it all up in his head. The clerk nodded, noted the land and smiled confidentially.

"You live in Danville?"

"Yeah."

"Deputy there? All right; I'll make out the papers and deliver 'em to you in a few days. You have the money."

Dave agreed. They parted with a handclasp and the clerk watched the lawman leave the office. His eyes were wide in speculation.

The ride back to Danville was made mostly in the dark. A small empire was his. Dave let his horse find the way, and thought about what he had done. Over nineteen-hundred acres of rich graze. Unquestionably the richest land in the Mesa country. It was a wonderful sensation. The restlessness was forever banished now. Even the sense of being an old rider, static and alone, left behind, sort of, was gone in the magic of being a land owner. More than a landowner; the landowner of Mesa Meadows; earliest feed in the uplands.

And then the grimness set in. Mesa Meadows was common ground to Bar Seven and Arrowhead. Between the two largest cow outfits in the country. And worse, Dave Reed would now be one of the hated, despised and ridiculed grangers. Clod-hoppers. Nesters. Homesteaders. The bridges would be burned behind him. Not just the camaraderie of the old riders, but of all riders, and all ranchers and all stockmen, except the very people he scorned himself; the other emigrants and squatters.

Danville was abed, except for Colton's Saloon, when he got back. The badge felt as heavy and conspicuous as a barn door, even in the dark. He pocketed it self-consciously before he rode in at the livery barn and put up his horse, crossed the road and clumped down the duckboards to the saloon. Dave didn't want to see Dick Newton that night, so he studied the crowd carefully before he went in. He didn't want to embarrass Dick, which would certainly happen if Newton set up the drinks for his new deputy, then fired him tomorrow for being a homesteader.

The longer he stood on the outskirts of the hilarious bedlam, the more uncomfortable and out of place he felt. As though, now, he was a spy, or something foreign to these cowmen and riders. He turned abruptly and left Colton's, went back down to the public corral on the north side of the livery barn and turned in.

It was a different man altogether, who lay there staring at the cobalt sky, from the rider who had lain there the night before. This new Dave Reed was a grave man, acutely conscious of the abyss he had deliberately opened up between the rest of the Mesa country and himself. He almost groaned, too, thinking of his old riding friends, and the way they would avoid him. How everything he, himself, had said and felt about clodhoppers, was now coming home to roost.

He writhed in his soogans. An outcast as surely as though he had hired out his gun. Beyond the pale of all the things he had formerly stood for; a foreigner in his own country. There was a strong yearning in him to throw it all up, forget what he had done, back out of it and never mention it. And then he thought of Lucy, and the old thoughts he had used to chase the blackness away with, on the ride back from Glenwood, flooded in. They'd have their own ranch. He'd build a log house in the meadows. A log barn and corrals, too. He made a face and swore into the darkness. There was no assuaging the discomfort he had known for two days, now. No respite. When he moved according to the dictates of the dissatisfaction within him, there appeared more and greater obstacles. If he didn't keep his homestead, he'd lose Lucy, surely, and, more than that, he'd grow grey as other old riders were doing, never forging ahead, and finally be forgotten in some remote line camp.

The fine lines around his grey eyes grew deeper and the set of his mouth, always a little flat anyway, grew flatter, more dogged and stubborn. His face was older, even in sleep.

Deputy Newton listened stonily. His usually placid, pinched features were blank. He squinted a tiny bit against the reflecting sunlight where it jumped off the table at him from the shiny new badge lying there amid the paperwork disorder. His feelings were mixed. Bitterness and irritation. He felt a little sorry, too, as he watched Dave trying to explain so hard. The rider gave him stare for stare, more in desperation than friendship.

"That's why I put the badge there, Dick. I'm probably all wrong in this thing. Usually am. Fifty a month wouldn't let me get married. Ninety and a badge will. With that, I could make this ranch for us. Well—the decision's yours, Dick."

Newton didn't say anything right away. He liked and respected Dave Reed, but asking Newton to condone homesteading, and on land that had been Bar Seven and Arrowhead graze for time out of mind, aside from the inevitable violence that was bound to erupt as soon as anyone established themselves in the meadows, put Dick, as the local representative of the law, in a bad spot. He couldn't appear to side with anything as controversial as a homesteader. He shrugged, pushed the badge away so the reflection wouldn't hit him in the eyes, and sighed audibly.

"You got me in a fix, Dave." He lowered his eyes and felt annoyance that Dave would do this to him. "There'll be trouble as sure as gawd made green apples. They'll kill you, boy." Another shrug, still with an averted face. "I'm sorry, Dave."

"Yeah." Dave got up heavy hearted, nodded shortly and walked out of the office. Dick watched him go and swore, pushed himself upright with jerky movements, pocketed the new badge and pursed his lips in a dry whistle that puckered the slate, cold blue of his eyes.

Dave went to Colton's Saloon with the cynical acceptance of his first rebuff fresh in his mind. He had an ale and sniffed at the familiar, stale smell of the place. The bartender lazily slapped at flies with a sour, damp bar-rag. There was no business. Too early. He sidled up where Dave was slouched and struck up a conversation.

"Freighters say they's a mob of nesters coming over the old Fort trail. Regular caravan of 'em."

Dave looked up. "Together?"

"Yeah. Said about fifty, sixty of 'em." The man laughed dryly, wagged his head and stroked his hand-some, auburn moustache. "George's sworn he'll shoot the first one comes over Arrowhead range. There'll be trouble this time, I expect."

Dave nodded. "Another ale." He was angry inside. The damned squatters were flocking in, and yet he was one of them, now. He knew George Marsters and Arrowhead felt strongly, and didn't blame them. All cowmen felt the same way. Soon he'd be right where Marsters said he'd kill homesteaders for trespassing. Mesa Meadows. His ranch. Dave Reed's ranch. The thought warmed him a little.

"Two Bar Seven riders in here last night. They said Bar Seven'd sure as hell go along with Arrowhead. Pardner—there's going to be all hell bust loose one of these days. You mark my words. The more of these

31

nesters come in, the closer she's gettin'. You watch."

Dave faced it then and there, for the second time. He had to improve the land according to the rules the man over at Glenwood had given him. That meant a house and other things. He couldn't hide what he'd done or he'd lose the land. The choice was still squarely in front of him. Forget it—or fight. He drank the ale non-stop and eyed the bartender bluntly. A good man to sound out. Better than Dick Newton, in a way. Setting his glass down he spoke.

"Well—they got a right to the land. They've got to work like the devil to earn it. It won't be easy for them, either. Anyway—they got the law behind them."

"The law," the bartender laughed harshly. "Not in cow country." Then he sucked in his breath, shot Dave a startled glance and went silent. His face fell back into its habitually wary, wooden expression. After a second of awkward silence, he picked up the damp rag and eased away, searching for flies again. Dave smiled wryly, laid a coin on the bar and walked out. He had his answer—again.

He stood in the shade of the saloon's overhang and tasted bitterness. He had just entered Colton's Saloon for the last time as a member of the honored fraternity of riders and cowmen, who used the place as their Danville headquarters. He swore under his breath, made his choice again, inwardly, and started down the scuffed plankwalk towards the mercantile establishment.

Old John Sebright showed him the rolls of murderous looking barbed wire he had in the storehouse. Sebright was uncomfortable. Dave was the first cowman who had asked to see the stuff and his flinty, hard face was screwed up as he figured requirements on a scrap of kindling. How many rolls would Mesa Meadows require for a three-strand fence?

Sebright shifted his weight, saying nothing, eyeing the compactly built man with the dusty black hat thumbed over his broad forehead. Sebright was a man enamored with the thought of profit, but he also hated a fight, and that barbed wire meant trouble and he knew it.

Dave looked up. "It'll take a lot of the stuff, John."

Sebright nodded glumly, wondering what Dave was going to fence in. "Yeah. Usually does. Freight's higher'n hell on it, too." He looked dispassionately at the glistening spools. "You want some, Dave?"

"Yeah. You got a wagon you could loan me?"

"I reckon." The watery eyes came up. "It ain't for Bar Seven is it?" Sebright knew it wasn't. He'd heard, through the grapevine, that Dave had been fired by Lester Mallow.

"Nope. It's for me."

"All right." Still glum, Sebright turned away. "Let's go harness the team."

The sun was high and scorchingly hot when Dave tooled John Sebright's wagon out of Danville with his load of shiny new wire. The merchant had the money—and the acutely uncomfortable feeling—that went with the sale. He watched Dave clear town and swing northwest, heading over the sweep of Bar Seven range. He winced as two early riders in from the ranches, reined up and sat their horses in startled immobility, twisting in the saddle and watching the wagon lurch along. Dave Reed with barbed wire!

Dave could feel the back of his neck, smoldering red, until he was clear of town. The rolls of wire shone like new silver. They glittered and sparkled like what they were, the confines of a new era and an invitation to war—and possibly death.

By the time he got to the meadows, Sebright's team was wringing wet and puffing. He was, too, before he had cached the last of the spools. His roping gloves were in shreds, his shirt torn and stiff with the salt of dried sweat. The perspiration was cold and unpleasant in spite of the heat. Each roll of wire he unloaded and trundled to the cache, put him in a little deeper. Too deep, in fact, ever to back out—unless it was feet first.

He piled brush until the shine was hidden. It had hurt his eyes as well as his conscience. A lot of his meager savings were in the wire but he had to get it up there before the news got around, otherwise he'd never be able to haul it over Bar Seven and Arrowhead range. Everything necessary had to come fast. He climbed back up into the wagon, full of scratches and aches, and started back.

At midnight he had made the last trip and unloaded the crosscut, the axes, the iron stove and piles of wood, then he took Sebright's wagon back, got his two horses and rode slowly, wearily, back to the meadows again. His back throbbed in outrage at the unaccustomed labor and the steady sweating had robbed him of a lot of saddle-accumulated weight. It was to be like this for some time to come. Less weight, a few more lines around the eyes and mouth, a darker sheen to the skin, and a more solemn look to the eyes.

He rode to Bar Seven the next day, braced for the meeting with Lester. The relief was very real when he was told Mallow had been called to Danville. Anne sent for Lucy, then went down to the barn to see the new milk cow the boys had brought in, and were breaking to stand.

Lucy looked at him in wonder. "What have you been doing, Dave? You look—well . . ."

He smiled wearily. "Yeah. Sort of used up, I reckon." He regarded the scratched, swollen hands distastefully and saw the filth on his clothing, too. "Lucy—I got us a ranch."

"Dave!"

He sobered at the enthusiasm in her voice. "Honey, I homesteaded Mesa Meadows."

She said his name again, but the sound was like air being punched out in horror. *"Dave!"*

He waited. Nothing more came. Just the name. He had a sinking sensation. "Lucy—I don't have any money. You can't save as a rider. We've got to have a home, honey. A decent one that'll be fit for visitors, and kids, and—all." It trailed off.

"Homesteading, Dave?"

"I know." There was thick exasperation in the words. "We all think about alike, on grangers, Lucy, but where in hell would we ever get the money to buy a ranch? Without a home, honey, we couldn't get married. Without land we'd have to be hired help some place. Takes land for cattle, Lucy." He watched her face and recoiled inwardly from the shock there. "I'm going to start on the house tomorrow." It was a wistful, hopeful addition to the other words, but her eyes didn't change expression.

"Oh," she said vaguely; then, "Where'll you put it?"

He answered a little listlessly. "Oh—by the falls. Below them, where the creek hits the meadows."

She nodded, knowing the spot well. That was where they had first kissed. She understood his wanting to put the house there all right, but there was the solid wall of rock, still formidable. Lucy had the inbred contempt for homesteaders that went with her environment. It was founded on uneasiness, as much as anything, because nothing seemed to stop them. Nothing. And they were a very real threat to the big cow outfits. Just knowing Dave had homesteaded made him appear different, suddenly. The glamour of his musical spurs, swaying gun, gently upcurving Stetson, and wide shoulders, were obscured considerably by his act of joining the ranks of the squatters.

Lucy didn't kiss him when he left. Anne waved gaily from the barn door, but the Bar Seven riders didn't even look up. Dave grimaced to himself. The word had spread fast. He knew what a pariah felt—if he had no knowledge of the word.

Chapter Three

GET OUT

The clerk from Glenwood brought over the deeds to the additional sections. He had made them out to show that Dave Reed had pre-emption rights. It wasn't legal and Dave knew it, but he was dedicated to an ideal now. He was gambling his life for land. The more land, the better odds. He gave the man his money and watched him ride away, then the labor began.

Before a building could grow, Dave had to cut the trees from the rim of purple forest across the meadows and snake them to the site with his saddle horses. Five days of toil that made him feverish with pain from the unaccustomed labor, grew to ten, then fifteen, and he had enough logs to make the bunkhouse, anyway, which he meant to live in until the rest of the logs for the main house were felled and ready. Each lonely day came and went. Lucy didn't ride over. Time meant nothing. Only daylight counted, and finally, with the little bunkhouse completed and the corrals up for his two horses, Dave set up housekeeping and took a day off. He sat on one of the benches he had made on the shady side of the squatty building, and looked somberly over the gradual drift of the land eastward from Mesa Meadows. But she didn't come.

He was lean and blackened by the fierce rays that had flayed him unmercifully—and miserable. But the aches and pains gradually left him. He was as fit as a cougar and as hard as steel. Only two things were recurrent, now; the everlasting sweat, and the low morale that plagued him even at night, when, dead tired, sleep wouldn't come. He had done it for Lucy. All of it. Thrown over his old life, old friends and haunts. Become almost a renegade in every cowman's eyes to make her a home—and she didn't ride up to see him, on their ranch.

He rode across the majestic meadows towards some distant specks he knew were cattle, in a depressed mood that told him he couldn't quit now, even though he heartily wanted to, because of Lucy. If he did, he'd have to leave the Mesa forever. Ridicule and contempt would drive him away.

The sun hadn't gathered its momentum of heat yet. The morning was still cool, with a soft, radiant light. He rode fairly close, reined up and watched the cattle. Bar Seven animals. They were slick, with big calves by their sides. He was still watching them when a faint rattle of rein-chains and the familiar sound of crickets in spade bits made him twist and look back.

Three riders were coming leisurely down across the meadow towards him. He turned his horse and waited. There was a thick, hard feeling in his throat. For fifteen days he had been left alone. That was over now. Arrowhead men. The apprehension that had lived with him constantly disappeared. Trouble was at hand, and he tensed to face it, but at least the apprehension that had been in him was relaxed in the face of certain trouble. Something he could see and hear.

He recognized Jerry Turk and George Marsters. The

third man, on a beautiful black gelding, was Roy Murdock, owner of Arrowhead. Short, broad and grizzled, Murdock, like Lester Mallow, had come to the Mesa country when both were young. He said little, moved deliberately and never bluffed. They reined up a few feet away without nodding and looked at Dave, then Murdock inclined his head slightly.

"Reed—I'm surprised you'd turn nester."

Dave said nothing, waiting. Murdock studied the whipcord frame, the bruised, swollen hands and the face grown thinner, older and more mature looking.

"You picked a bad spot to squat. This land's part of the out-range. Common graze for Bar Seven and Arrowhead. You're trespassing." The last words had a dry sound.

Dave didn't blink an eye. "Mesa Meadows used to be public land. Used to be. Now I own it. Neither Bar Seven or Arrowhead need it. I do."

Murdock didn't answer right away. He relaxed with his hands in plain sight, crossed over the saddlehorn. He was armed, as was Jerry Turk. George's gun sagged close to his thigh and, of the three, he looked the most hostile. Murdock nodded again, slightly. His features were cold and relentless.

"You going to run cattle here?"

Dave almost smiled. He had no money left to buy them with. That was his dream, of course, but when, or how, he'd get cattle was beyond him right then. He told Murdock none of this; just shrugged.

"Well—you going to fence?"

"I reckon, some time. Don't have anything to fence in,

39

now, and it's getting late, but I may start fencing this Fall."

Murdock nodded again. With resignation, this time. "All right Reed, you're bringing trouble on yourself. I reckon you know that."

"Listen, Murdock. You're welcome any time, up here. You and the other Arrowhead men. Same goes for Bar Seven. But don't ever forget you're trespassing when you come here uninvited." He smiled wryly. "Trouble? I don't think you're that type, Murdock. Maybe I'm wrong. I hope not."

George cleared his throat and spat. Murdock shot him a glance that killed whatever the foreman was going to say, then he faced back towards Dave.

"You're wrong, Reed. Dead wrong. Arrowhead's used this land for a long time. So has Bar Seven. You're asking for trouble in what you're doing here. You'll get it." He started to lift the reins when Dave spoke, hesitated and didn't move farther, the dull luster of his eyes cold and uncompromising.

"Listen, Murdock. I don't know how you got your start, but I'll bet it was about like I'm doing. If you'll be fair, you'll understand why I'm doing this. It'll be uphill every inch of the way without your opposition. Yours and Bar Seven's. Sure—this has been part of your out-range, but hell, it wouldn't stay that way forever. If I hadn't homesteaded the meadows, someone else would've. You know that. Better to have a cowman here than a common squatter."

Murdock's eyes were sardonic. "The meadows are early spring feed-grounds, Reed. If you wanted to homestead, you could've picked any land, anywhere else in the Mesa, and Arrowhead wouldn't have bothered you. You still can. But don't figure for a second I'll let you take my early feed without a fight. If you were reasonable you'd understand this."

He watched Dave's face, saw no answer coming back, regarded the homesteader solemnly for a moment, then nodded again as he spoke.

"Make it easy on all of us, Reed. Get out!"

The reins went up and sideways, the black horse turned gracefully and Reed sat still, watching the three men jog easily over his land, heading back the way they had come. He was still watching them when they hesitated a little way from his squatty log house and looked at it, then resumed their homeward trip.

Four more days of solitude. Dave built a log shelter on to his corrals behind the bunkhouse and made a set of cupboards over the stove inside. It was while he was fitting the slab doors that his next visitor came down over the meadows towards the house. This time he saw the rider long before the horse was in close. He went outside and waited, leaning against an upright, eyes squinted against the sunglare, searching for recognition. The horseman came on slowly, tall and slightly bent in the saddle, his head never wavering from an inspection of the bunkhouse and corrals.

It was Deputy Dick Newton. He swung down and tied his horse in the lee-shade and stomped off the summer dust, twin guns swaying rhythmically with his jerky movements. He thumbed back his Stetson and cuffed the sweat off his forehead with a sigh.

41

"Hotter'n the devil, Dave."

"Yeah. Sit down." They both sank back against the log wall on benches.

Newton's eyes flickered quizzically over the house, then drifted back to the slow sweep of the great breadth of grassy land. He had a brooding, thoughtful look on his pinched face. "Dave—Arrowhead been to see you yet?"

"Yeah. Murdock, George and Jerry Turk."

"Yeah, well—there's some hot blood in the country over you taking up this land."

"Not surprised," Dave said dryly.

"No, me neither. You knew what you were doing, I reckon. Anyway, I told you there'd be trouble."

"I expected it, Dick, but, dammit, how else can a man get a start?"

Newton shook his head to fling off the sweat and used his sleeve to mop at the residue. "You're right, there. No question about it. Kind of funny, too."

"What?"

"Well—two things. First, these fellows know a man's got to strike out for himself sometime—if he's the kind that wants to—and yet they'll fight tooth and fang to keep him from making a go of it. All right for them, but all wrong for anybody else." Dave nodded, saying nothing. "And the other funny thing is old Lester."

"Lester Mallow?"

"Yeah. Murdock's screaming like a wounded eagle. He wants war. So's George and a lot of other folks who've got no business in the mess at all. But Bar Seven hasn't said a thing. Murdock nailed me on the

42

road and cussed you out good. I asked him what Lester had said, and he got red as a beet and cussed Bar Seven as much as you."

"Huh!"

Dick nodded slowly, with puckered eyebrows. "Yeah, seems Lester's for keeping hands off for a while, but I wouldn't be too easy on that score if I was you." The deputy swung his head arid looked squarely at Dave. "Funny though, isn't it?"

Dave nodded in perplexity. "Yeah, funny as hell." He told Dick about the brief, stormy last meeting he and Lester had in the Bar Seven office.

Newton scratched his thin beak of a nose. "Well— maybe it's Lucy. Maybe she's made Lester keep off you. Lucy or Anne."

"I doubt it," Dave said morosely, not looking at Newton.

The deputy turned again and studied Dave thoughtfully, saying nothing until he had speculated on the hollow way Dave had said the last words. "She been up to see you lately?"

"Nope. Lucy hasn't ridden over since I came up here." Dave had an idea and swung his head quickly. "Do me a favor, will you, Dick?"

"Sure. Anything except hire you back as a deputy. What is it?"

"Pack a note to her at Bar Seven."

"Yeah. Glad to." Newton fished for his tobacco sack. "Dave—I figured we had a talk coming; that's why I rode up here today. First off, I don't know what you thought when I let you turn in the badge. Maybe you

43

figured I was against you like the rest of them, for homesteading. Well—I got no use for squatters, but this is different. Anyway, there's another side to this thing. If I'd kept you on, the cowmen'd of gotten my job for having you working for me."

"I know."

Dick lit and inhaled. "Well—there's something you don' know, too. It's a secret between you and me. I'm all for you in this thing. You got the legal right, and I think you're smart for striking out on your own. Besides, you're a cowman, not a damned clod-hopper. I used to be a rider, too, and there's no future in it. Well— I can help you a damned sight more by keeping my eyes and ears open, than by openly siding with you. I wanted to be sure you understood this."

"Thanks, Dick." There was more than gratitude in Dave then. It was the first word of encouragement he'd had in close to a month of desolation. It leavened the feeling of being an outcast and made him gravely pleased. He smiled, something he hadn't done in two weeks. Newton's next words jarred him out of the feeling of mellowness, though.

They were hard words, softly spoken.

"This isn't all talk, Dave, that Arrowhead's putting out. They're out to get you off the meadows. It'll come pretty soon, too. You're worse than a squatter to them. You're a sort of cowman renegade. A rider gone traitor—or something. They figure you're worse than a regular nester." He squashed out his cigarette on the packed ground. "You're a long way from Danville, Dave, and alone. Don't make any mistakes. They're out

44

to clean you out of here by hook or crook. I'll help you all I can, but I got no way of knowing when they'll come at you—or how. Keep your ears to the ground, boy. That's what I rode up here to tell you."

He stood up and stretched with those quick, darting movements that were a part of him. "Now, doggonit, let's eat, I'm hungrier'n a bitch-wolf."

They ate, and Dave wrote his note to Lucy and watched Dick ride slowly back over the shimmering land, with the letter in his shirt pocket. He felt a lot better, and thoroughly defiant. The sadness that was in him over Lucy's failure to show up, was almost smothered in the resolve to fight for what was his, in spite of the solid doubt whether what he had done was ever going to be worth the stigma and trouble it was bringing.

He shoved off his bench and went over to the pole corrals to care for his horses. There was little about Dave Reed, now, that there had been there thirty days before. The almost dandified bearing of a top rider was buried under layers of sunburn, faded, torn clothing, and a gait that spoke of a man used to walking.

Even the silvered spurs were gone from his boots and hung forlornly on a nail inside the log house. Just the gun remained, thonged to his leg, a dead weight that galled, but he couldn't dispense with it, either. And then, when he needed it, it lay flat against him, available, yet useless.

He was making a little bleeder-ditch from the creek that meandered across the meadows, trenching the water so that it would spread and irrigate the scorched feed, using a shovel with the sureness of a man who had acquired the knack, when four men rode slowly towards him from the rim of sentinel pines on the far side of the meadow, behind him. He didn't hear them until they were less then six-hundred feet away, and then it was too late. He whirled, still clutching the shovel. The men came on, stony-faced and deliberate. George Marsters was in the lead, his vandyke beard a coppery frame for the swarthiness of his dark, heavy features. Dave recognized. Arrowhead riders. He said nothing as they approached; just watched them come up.

George reined up, lowered his rein hand and slouched, staring down at Dave. "You didn't take Murdock's advice, did you, Dave?"

"What advice?" He knew, though.

"About getting out."

"No, George, I didn't." He knew too, this was it, by the hostile looks. Throwing caution to the winds, he let the shovel drop. A lone man, dirty, bedraggled, and as lean as a lobo wolf, afoot before the Arrowhead riders—four of them—cold-eyed and intent.

"Like I told Murdock, George, when you and Jerry, there, were with him. You're trespassing."

George's head wagged slowly from side to side. "No, you got that backwards. You're the one that's trespassing, Dave. You was told to get off the meadows. You didn't do it. Now we're here to clear you out." He jerked a savage thumb towards the burly log house. "You and that out-house eye-sore you made."

Dave said nothing. He was helpless before them. The gun at his hip was useless, unless he wanted to go up

46

against a suicidal stacked deck, which he didn't. He knew it, too, and stared at each rider in turn, saw nothing but enmity, and shrugged.

"George—turn those horses around and get off the meadow." Dave knew how hollow and ridiculous it sounded when he said it.

George's hand flickered. A gun peeked down at Dave. The foreman's voice was thin and quiet. "Use your piggin'-string, Josh."

A pock-marked cowboy swung down, jerked a short rope from behind his cantle and walked forward, eyes wide and wary. There was just the small music of the man's spurs in the silence, before George spoke again.

"You're worse than the others, Dave. You're a lousy traitor. You know better. Damned emigrants don't. There's no excuse for you. You had your chance. Murdock told you to go somewhere else and squat." The Arrowhead rider stood a little to one side of Dave, hesitating. George nodded brusquely. "Tie his hands behind him, don't bother with his legs."

Dave's anger seethed. It looked like they intended to hang him. Lynch him on his own land. The rider was bending forward, looking at Dave's hands, when the flash of a fist whirled towards him. He saw it, but way too late. The knuckles exploded under his ear like a battering ram. Dave heard a voice he recognized as Jerry Turk's, raised in a falsetto cry of alarm. He was spinning away, clawing for his gun, when the world blew apart in his face and the sky fell on him.

There was a faint glow left in the twilight when Dave opened his eyes. His head felt like a glass window that someone kept dropping steel balls against. Each heart beat made the skull shiver like it would burst open. Acute pain danced into his mind from just behind the eyeballs. He sat up, felt the awful swelling where a bullet had gouged along his cheek-bone and ripped through his right ear. He got up slowly, stood wide-legged, until the agony receded a little, then went towards the house, half blinded and staggering.

Then he stopped several hundred feet away and surveyed the Arrowhead's work. The bunkhouse was gone. He went on, then veered off and washed his face and head in the creek and lay down on the thin fringe of green grass, letting the earth suck at the fever in him, until he felt better. The urge to sob was great. He swore instead. Only one force on earth could have so completely demolished his burly log house. Dynamite. The Arrowhead had come well prepared.

Resting his head in the grass for a long time, Dave finally twisted a little and looked behind him. Mesa Meadows was a barren place again. Still and barren, with a hushed atmosphere of violence and melancholy strangely merged into an almost tangible sense of withheld breath. The bunkhouse was gone completely, the great logs broken and scattered like splinters. He caught the dull realization fully, like a mule's kick over the kidney, and let his head fall back into the coolness of the grass again.

Sleep overwhelmed him, but it was a slumber induced by shock, and the anguish of his torn flesh and shattered ear. The agony awakened him when the

48

sky was sprinkled with stars. He had one horse left. The other one had evidently jumped the corral fence when the house went up. He saddled up and rode towards Danville. The ride was a nightmare of trickling blood, semi-consciousness and purple darkness, never clearly remembered.

Danville's doctor was a man named Billings. He was a rough humored, heavy-bellied man who rarely asked questions. He appraised the purple, mangled flesh and shook his head negatively in shock. "Come in, son. Sit there, on that stool. Lord! That'll be a hell of an ear left." He went to work, still shaking his head. "Whoever did it, came as close as you can come."

"How about the face?"

"Well—that'll heal in time. A few scars, is all. That and powder burns. How in hell he missed the bone I'll never know. There'll be plenty of scars, sure, but I've seen worse. A lot of the ear is just hanging. It'll have to be trimmed off."

When it was over, Dave gingerly explored the massive bandage. The pain wasn't as bad as before. In fact, Doctor Billings had put something over the raw meat that had a soothing, cool feeling. Just the dull, insistent throbbing persisted in Dave's head. He thanked the doctor, paid him and left.

Chapter Four

BULLETS AND BANDAGES

Danville was half quiet; the clamor from Colton's Saloon droned into the night. Dave stood in the shadows of a weak, moist moon, and watched the strollers out for a breath of coolness after the sunblast of the day. He squinted at the myriad horses before the saloon. There were few Arrowhead mounts. George's massive bay wasn't around. He shuffled across the stained roadway and went back to his horse, where he had tied it to a picket fence in back of town. He was in the saddle, heading back over Bar Seven, but slightly south-west, towards Arrowhead, and didn't see the doctor come out of his house and hike directly towards the small square of light that lay, orange-yellow, on the roadway outside the deputy's office.

Dick was idly regarding a messy pile of paperwork with a disdainful expression, when the doctor entered. He smiled absently and waved towards the bench across the room from him.

"What's the matter, Doc? You look like you just saw a ghost."

"Darn near, at that. You know that Dave Reed fellow? Used to ride for Bar Seven?"

"Sure. What about him?"

"I've only seen him a couple of times myself, or I wouldn't have recognized him."

Dick's face froze. He didn't move in the chair. Just

stared at the doctor with a glassy, dangerous look, and nodded. "Go on."

"He just left my office. Lord! Someone shot damned near his whole ear off, and half his face." The doctor shook his head against Newton's offering of the tobacco sack. "He's a mess."

"Gunshot?"

"Sure. I've seen enough of them to know, Lord knows. Went along his cheek-bone, under the eye, tore the flesh all to hell, then went through his right ear and ripped a lot of the cartilage away."

Dick relaxed slowly, bent his head and made a cigarette, then lit it and exhaled. The peculiar, tawny look in his sunken eyes didn't escape the doctor. "He's gone?"

"Yeah. Paid me and left. Just like that. That man's made of iron. The thing must be giving him hell."

"He's iron, all right," Dick said quietly. "I don't think he knows how much is iron, himself. Did he tell you how it happened?"

"No, and I didn't ask."

"Don't blame you." Dick smoked idly for a moment. "Which way'd he go?"

"Headin' across Bar Seven, the last I saw him. Had his horse tied over on the west side of town somewhere."

"Towards Arrowhead, maybe?"

"In the general direction, I'd say, Dick." The doctor caught on and scowled. "I've heard the talk, Dick. He's the lad who homesteaded up on Mesa Meadows, isn't he?" Dick nodded. "Well—do you suppose Bar Seven or Arrowhead jumped him?"

"I'd say yes to the last one, Doc, if I was guessing.

51

There's been a lot of war talk lately, by Arrowhead."

"Yes, I know. Rumors. I've heard them. After all, this is a small town."

"Yeah," Dick agreed lazily. "Too small, I think, sometimes. Too small and quick tempered."

The doctor arose. "Well—are you going after him, Dick?"

"What for?"

"He's in no shape to be riding around. If an infection would set in, it might easily be fatal."

Dick inhaled a big gust of smoke and let it trickle past his nostrils. "In the morning, Doc. Really, though, it's none of my business what Dave does—unless he breaks a law or something. I can't scoop him up just for his own health, unless he wants to come in. You know that."

"Yes, but hell; the man shouldn't be loose with that wound."

Dick smiled indulgently. "All right, Doc. I'll ride up and talk to him tomorrow."

The doctor left and Dick shoved out of his chair with an angry blasphemy. His neck muscles were corded as he punched cartridges into the few empty loops in his shell-belt. War had come. The war that Dick Newton knew was coming and had been waiting for. Furious, there was a little exhilaration in him, too. Sitting around Danville day in and day out, or hunting for some nester's strayed milk cow, had galled. He gave the doctor ample time to get back home before he blew down the chimney of his office lamp, and went quickly down the plankwalk towards the liverybarn. The ring of his spurs was insistent and loud in his hurry.

At the barn, Dick Newton got his horse, saddled it under the surprised eye of the nighthawk, stepped up and swung out of town, south-west, over Bar Seven range. He rode slowly, grave-faced and thoughtful. He thought he knew Dave Reed pretty well. In fact, he and Lucy had discussed him for over an hour—with the wall of Lucy's sickroom between them—that very afternoon. Now, he wondered if he—or Lucy either for that matter—knew Dave as well as they thought. Badly shot up and in agony, he had gone riding into the night again, instead of seeking comfort and help as well as the attention for his wound the doctor said he needed. The night was spent. Dick could smell the tiny chill that comes before dawn as he rode. It would be daylight before he got to Arrowhead.

But Dave was ahead of Dick. False dawn was spreading out feelers of pink light when he came into the vast valley that held the Arrowhead buildings. He sat his horse in the pine fringe, motionless and feverish in the coolness, waiting. It didn't take long. The riders trooped out of the cook shack fumbling with their tobacco sacks. Dave counted them. Seven, all told. Eight, counting Roy Murdock, who wasn't among them. He saw George detail the men to jobs and raged when Jerry Turk and a half-breed cowboy headed for the corrals, roped horses, saddled up and rode out of the yard together, northward, towards Mesa Meadows. He wanted George worse than any of the others.

Dave swung his horse. He knew the back trails well enough. Keeping ahead of the Arrowhead riders wasn't hard. They were riding leisurely. He smiled to himself. Undoubtedly, Arrowhead was convinced the coyotes and buzzards were feasting on his remains.

Dave picked his spot well and waited. He didn't move even after he heard their voices. Not until he heard the horses' hooves, then he drew his gun, cocked it and jumped his horse out, athwart the trail. The voices snapped off in mid-sentence. Dave had one fast flash of two startled, slack-mouthed faces, and made a hideous smile that was deflected downward by the bulge of the scarlet, angry flesh under the bandage.

"Turk."

The 'breed threw himself sideways, off his horse. Turk flung a ragged curse in a voice scratchy with terror at the apparition before him and lashed a hand for his gun. The dual explosions were close, then a third shot ripped the trail silence and Jerry went off his lunging, frightened colt, backwards, literally knocked out of the saddle by the crashing impact of the second bullet, which took him at close quarters and high in the chest.

Dave's cocked .45 pinned the 'breed down. He quieted his horse and faced the rider. "Well? You buying in?"

The cowboy shook his head emphatically. "No. Not me," he said loudly, through stiff lips. "I'm new on the Arrowhead."

Dave nodded. He didn't recognize the man. He hadn't been with the four riders who had jumped him the day before and left him for dead.

"All right. Put Turk back on his horse and take him back." The 'breed nodded without making a move to get up. "Tell George I'm looking for him. Him and Murdock."

"Sure, I'll tell 'em."

"Toss that gun into the brush." The Arrowhead man obeyed with stiff fingers. Dave nodded again, twisted backwards in the saddle and spurred out of sight among the trees. The excitement made his head ache again. He rode slowly through the forested vastness until he came to a creek, unsaddled, lay down, face forward, and patted the cool water over his head until the drowsiness and relief conspired to make him sleep again, this time with fewer awakenings, and in a stupor induced by complete mental and physical exhaustion.

Dave was lost in the realm of unconsciousness when Dick Newton swung down before Murdock's house and eyed the broken, gory body of Jerry Turk lashed over his horse where the Arrowhead riders and their boss were standing around in thick silence. Dick understood in a flash. He was too late, after all. He took it all in as he crossed the yard. Murdock nodded absently to him and waved a hand at the dead man.

"It's Jerry. Reed did it. Sauric, there, was with him. Reed jumped them on the trail."

Dick faced the short, stocky 'breed. "You Sauric?" The rider inclined his head, saying nothing. His large, dark eyes were alive and intense. "Who shot first?"

"Both about the same time."

Dick sighed. "Where were you?"

"I went off my horse. This Reed, he come out on to the trail and called Jerry. I jumped off. Too damned close to Jerry."

"Then what?"

"Then I stayed down."

"Didn't you try to draw on Reed?"

"No, he covered me. Said did I want in. I told him, no. I was a new Arrowhead man. He nodded at me, said to take the body back and tell George and Murdock he was comin' after them."

Dick turned his back on the 'breed and faced Murdock. The rancher's face was pale and set in harsh lines. His eyes were like ice. "Well—Murdock. How'd it happen?"

Murdock shook his head. "Damned if I know. Reed's gone crazy. Riding around shooting Arrowhead riders."

"Sure," Dick said slowly and sarcastically. "He's been on those meadows for a month or so, and bothered no one. He just went crazy this morning about dawn. This morning he got out of bed and took a notion to wipe out Arrowhead. You want to talk and make sense, or don't you, Murdock? I don't give a damn which you do, personally." Murdock's face showed flinty indecision. Dick prompted him. "What happened at Mesa Meadows, yesterday?"

Murdock's eyes clouded slightly. He sucked in his underlip and nodded twice. "I warned Reed about a week ago. He was on Arrowhead and Bar Seven outrange."

Murdock's head bobbed. "Yes. Yesterday, George, and a few of my boys went up there to see if Reed was still around. He was, and went for his gun. He got shot."

Dick stared at the rancher for a long time. There was an awkward silence. George edged over, angry eyed and

56

challenging. "Well," he said thickly, "what are you going to do about Jerry?"

Dick took his gaze from Murdock and lashed it over the Arrowhead foreman. He had never liked George Marsters. It was like flint on steel between them. The deputy's nostrils contracted once. "Nothing. Not a damned thing, George. Jerry got a fair shake according to your rider there. It was a fair fight, near as I can see, and Jerry came off low man."

George swore sulphurously. "Siding with Reed, Dick?"

Dick's eyes flamed viciously. "Siding with no one. The law don't play favorites. You heard the 'breed. He said they shot together, or something like that. That's a fair fight."

Before the foreman could get his words organized, the deputy leaned a little towards him. "And I'm going to tell Arrowhead something, too, for that matter. If Dave Reed comes to my office in Danville and swears out a complaint, I'll be back to see you again."

Murdock's anger was cold. The rational, murderous, crafty kind of anger. He nodded curtly. "Dick—you're making a mistake. Reed had no right to do what he did. I have friends in Glenwood, don't forget that."

Newton was fighting to control himself. Murdock saw the battle flags flying in his eyes and gave stare for stare. "Don't take that tack, Murdock. I get paid to do a job. I doubt if any friends you got in Glenwood'll back you against the law. Sheriff Stanley isn't for sale, either." The rancor subsided a little but the bitterness stayed. "I hope Dave comes in and makes a complaint.

This damned mess has gone far enough."

Murdock's answer came right back, flat and succinct. "He'll never live to get to Danville, Dick."

Deputy Newton turned slowly to the Arrowhead riders. "You boys heard that. That's a threat. Remember it. Remember who said it, too. You'll be asked about it before this thing is over with." He turned jerkily, walked over to his horse and swung up and rode out of Arrowhead yard without another glance at the men watching him depart. He was seething inwardly as he reined for the trail to Mesa Meadows, and didn't see the 'breed rider touch George's arm.

"I want my time, foreman. I ain't hiring into no war with the law."

Dick wasn't alone in his destination. Dave had awakened, saddled up and struck out for the same place. There was nothing to go there for, but the pull of the meadows—his land—carried him to the edge of the forest, where he sat his horse and squinted at the lone horseman he saw sitting before the blasted log bunkhouse, slump shouldered, eyeing the wreckage.

Dave recognized Dick Newton, but he didn't ride out to meet him. Instinctively he knew that Dick had found out about Jerry Turk. He was satisfied with the way it had been. Self-defense. Still, he sat back warily and felt the first stirrings of the leeriness of an outlaw. A silent, lobo rider of the dim back-trails. He wondered when Dick dismounted, appeared to be writing something, swung back up and rode southward, without a backward glance, down the meadow towards Danville.

Still wondering at sunset Dave let the shadows

lengthen a little before he crossed the open land, went where the deputy had been and found an unsigned note. He read it with a wry smile. Dick Newton was no fool. He had known Dave would return. The scrap of paper told him that Lucy had been sick in bed—had the Spanish measles, whatever they were. That's why she hadn't ridden over. Also, if Dave would swear out a complaint against Arrowhead for blowing up his house, trespassing and attempted murder, Dick would arrest George and Roy Murdock.

Dave pocketed the note and smiled into the gloom as he headed southward, too, but not towards Danville. Only as far as Bar Seven, where he tied his horse in the shadow of a scrub-oak thicket, shed his spurs and went towards the house from the rear, until he was at Lucy's bedroom window. It had never occurred to him that something might be wrong with the girl, and no one would bring him the news of her illness.

There was a lamp burning. He saw the girl lying in bed reading and he had his head through the window before she saw him.

"Dave!"

"Howdy, honey."

"Oh—Dave!" Lucy twisted in the bed and blew into the lamp mantle. The room darkened except for the watery, opalescent moonlight. "Dick left me a note. I wondered why you didn't ride up." It was a classical understatement and he knew it.

"Honey—I've wanted to so badly. These measles . . ." She was looking at the stiff bandage with horror in her eyes. "Dave—what's happened? Dick wouldn't tell me anything. Said I shouldn't get upset. Dave, what happened to your face?"

"Arrowhead jumped me. I got nicked. It's a beauty." He was smiling down at her, straddling a little chair with his arms locked over the back. "Would you sky off from marrying a squatter with one ear?" There was an undertone of irony in his banter.

She didn't answer the question. "Kiss me, Dave. It's terrible being here flat on my back when—when—" It trailed off and died unsaid. He left his chair and knelt by her bed. She ran a gentle hand over the bandage. There were real tears filming over the lover's stardust in her eyes. The kiss was his assurance. It was full of her longing for him. He pushed back and locked one dark hand over hers.

"Lucy—I thought, maybe, when you didn't show up, it was because I homesteaded. You know—the last time I was here, honey—well—you didn't kiss me when I left."

"Dave—you didn't understand. It wasn't that. I was scared. It took my breath away, what you'd done. Homesteading was bad enough, darling, but Mesa Meadows—don't you understand? I know what would happen. If Bar Seven didn't jump you, Arrowhead was bound to. I was scared for you Dave—for us. I didn't mean it all the way you thought—not kissing you—I mean." Her eyes were wide and the lean, worn look of him was like a dagger in her heart. "And then I got sick. It almost drove me crazy, Dave, worrying about you up on the meadows alone, between Bar Seven and Arrowhead." She fought valiantly, stubbornly against the tears. There was the iron of Lester in her, as well as the great understanding of Anne.

Dave sighed and made a wry face. He sought for something to jar her thoughts off their troubles. Seeing her cry, hurt far worse than the bullet-shattered face he wore. "Tell me something, honey. Why hasn't Lester been up with the Bar Seven riders?"

It worked. She frowned through the tears. It threw the graceful saddle of her nose into a piquant squint with fine wrinkles. "Anne and I talked about that. It's odd, Dave, Dad won't discuss you, or what you've done, with anyone. If Mother or I bring it up, he turns on his heels and walks away. He did the same thing when Roy Murdock rode into the yard with his riders, a week or two back. I thought there was going to be a fight for a while. Dad turned his back on Murdock in the middle of the talk, and walked away. Roy called after him and Dad ordered him off the ranch and threatened to shoot him out of the saddle if he didn't get off and stay off."

Dave showed his amazement. "The devil. I can't understand it."

The girl nodded, tears forgotten now. "Murdock was fighting mad. So were his riders. Dad called out the Bar Seven boys and Murdock rode off. It's hard to figure out, Dave. Haven't any Bar Seven riders been to the meadows?"

Dave shook his head. "Not a one, Lucy, that I know of. Dick told me Murdock had talked to your Dad and was mad at him. It's damned peculiar—isn't it?"

Lucy nodded absently, then held up her arms towards

61

him. "Come around on the other side of the bed and lie down beside me. You look tired."

He went readily enough and smiled at her when he spoke. "No, not tired. I slept most of the day." He lay down, stretched out and marveled at anything as soft as her bed. And promptly fell asleep. Once, it seemed there were voices, somewhere in the shadow world of oblivion. But it must have been a part of the pattern of unconsciousness, because when he opened his eyes Lucy was drawing her arm from under his head. The movement had jarred him awake.

He blinked at her. "Must have dozed off."

"Well," she said tartly. "Your head weighs a ton. I've learned one thing tonight. I'll never let you go to sleep on my arm again." She tossed her head with a mischievous smile. "Honey—there's some food on the dresser. Why don't you eat it, and wash in the bowl there. It'll make you feel better."

The more he ate of the meat, the more his hunger appalled him. He was famished. Finished, he washed gingerly and wondered that the headache no longer troubled him. He turned his back to the little dresser, crossed to the chair again and sprawled on it with a solemn look at the beautiful, voluptuous outline under the light sheeting.

"Lucy—Lester's not always wrong."

She looked up surprised, and laughed. "No. No one is. But why Dad?"

He shrugged. "Oh—it's just something I thought of. But he's sure a hard man to figure out."

"Until you have the key, Dave."

"You have it?"

She nodded. "Yes, I think so."

"Well, then—tell me something. What's his attitude in this mess?"

Lucy shook her head. "No, I won't tell you that. I'm not even sure I know it myself. I think I do, but I'm not sure. Anyway, if he doesn't want it known, I shouldn't tell on him, should I?"

Dave grunted. "I reckon not." He got up, dismissing the thought of Lester Mallow from his mind. "We almost had a home on our ranch, Lucy. Damned near."

"What do you mean 'damned near'?"

"Well—I built a log house. Arrowhead blew it up. Anyway, I just figured to use it for a bunkhouse someday."

"Dave!"

He nodded, smiling at her wide-eyed look. "I didn't see them do it, but I'm sure they did." He was moving towards the window again.

"That's why I want to get out of here before dawn. Murdock'll be after me like a catamount." He was thinking of Jerry Turk but didn't mention him.

"Dave—go see Dick. You have rights, darling. He'll know what to do—legally."

He smiled again, ruefully this time. "I'm sure he will, honey." But he didn't say he'd go.

Lucy looked at him indignantly. "You're not going without kissing me, are you?"

"I reckon not—but I should."

She understood even as he went back closer to the bed. "Don't be foolish. I didn't kiss you—well—like I

63

told you. I was too horrified even to think about it."

Dave knelt beside the bed. "Well—I could be horrified that you've got the measles, too. Besides, it isn't healthy to be kissing you now."

"You ape," Lucy said savagely, pulling him down to her. "I'm about over the silly measles anyway. Now kiss me!"

He did, with the full rapture he felt, allowing his cracked, chapped lips to revel in the coolness of her touch, until the breath that glanced off his upper lip had an awry, ragged whisper to it, then he got up slowly, grinning wickedly, and ducked out of the window with Lucy's command to return the following night in his ears.

The horse was drowsing lazily when Dave came up, unbuckled his spurs from the rigging D, strapped them on, felt the cinch and swung up. The night was well advanced.

Dave had a vague notion as he reined around out of the scrub-oak thicket and rode into the shadow world of eerie patchwork, made by the trees and brush around him. He would ride to Danville, like Lucy said and see Dick. If he was wanted for the killing of Jerry Turk, then he'd give himself up to Dick, but mainly, he'd see if there wasn't a peaceful way to halt the ebb-tide of violence that was temporarily rolled back upon itself, hesitating, before it gathered momentum and rolled outward again, steeping him in the violence of an all-out war with Arrowhead.

But Dave was too late. Not only too late, but he was to learn that Murdock was a deadly enemy, as well as a wily one. He was clearing the last of the scrub-oak shadows, riding eastward and almost beside a huge old witness-tree, left lonely and forlorn after its fellow pines had been felled, scarred with the symbols of long dead surveyors, when the night opened its cloak of pale purple to allow a lean, ferocious tongue of flame to fly out at him. The thunder of the carbine and its lethal echo went chasing each other endlessly over the dead land.

Dave felt his shirt jerk wildly away from his back, then he flung himself behind the old witness-tree and lay still, breathing hard; listening to his startled horse drum off into the near distance, before it overcame the fright and went to cropping grass.

Dave held his six-shooter lightly, cocked and riding balanced in his fist. Carefully, he eased his head around the base of the tree and waited. There was no sound. If the assassin had been sure of his work, or frightened off, there would have been the sound of a running horse. There wasn't. Some alarmed birds shrilled indignantly in the brush nearby, but they subsided eventually, and the watery night, with its still shadows and silence, closed in again.

Dave guessed that the bushwhacker was uncertain. The man must have thought his bullet had struck home, and yet he also had sufficient doubts to stay where he was, puzzling, perhaps, and being prudently watchful. The fall, in the darkness, may have looked realistic enough. It certainly had the spontaneity of a direct hit.

Dave's face was a death mask, with its large patch of white cloth and the glittering, grey eyes that raked the range for sign of movement. He began a slow and laborious backward edging that took him, eventually, to a clump of mesquite. Here he hunched forward flat, and watched the old tree. He guessed the ambusher to be an Arrowhead rider and was incredulous that Murdock would go to such extremes as to have men watching each place he might be. He didn't know Roy Murdock or George Marsters as well as he thought. Dawning caution went through him. He knew Murdock's reputation. In the Timberline they said he never bluffed. Dave made a wry face. That was a conservative description of the man. Ruthless was better. He knew also, that the gun shot must have carried to the Bar Seven, and ground his teeth. Lucy would hear, and be certain he had walked into an ambush. His annoyance grew, too, as the seconds ticked off and the ambusher didn't show himself. They were both pinned down by the other, and Dave couldn't lie there until dawn.

Then there was a daring, swift blue of movement. Dave's finger curled on the trigger and the gun lowered until it was almost butted to the ground. A large rock dropped out of the night, close to the witness-tree. Dave smiled coldly, contemptuously. Several more rocks fell closer, then an interval of stillness made dread and tension weave a spell of blanketing fear over the lonely, moonlighted area around the old tree.

Dave finally located the man. He was getting more confident, hunching over and wary, but showing more of himself as he came forward. The carbine glistened dully, moistly, in his hands. He held his fire and studied the bushwhacker until he was close to the tree, then he

66

recognized him as the man George had called Josh. The rider Dave had bowled over before George had shot him. He leveled the .45 squarely, aligned the man down the stubby barrel with slow care, and eased back on the trigger. The gun jumped convulsively in his hand. Rocked back against his thumb-pad and made his ears ring.

Almost instantly, the carbine exploded again, but it was a nerveless, dead hand that recoiled in death around the trigger. Dave saw the man fall and lie threshing as he shoved off the ground and ran forward, rolled Josh over with a boot-toe, saw the puckered hole in his forehead, grabbed the carbine from the convulsive fingers and raced through the night where his horse was still grazing.

There was exultation and iron in Dave as he whirled the horse and rode deeper into the bushy areas of Bar Seven. Murdock wanted war; all right, he would have it. Lucy's idea of seeing Dick Newton returned. He loped towards Danville, an Arrowhead carbine balanced across his lap, twisted backwards in the saddle, looking over the pall of dead land.

Somewhere, a long way behind Dave, a man called out. Then another. Lamps appeared in the darkness from the erupting Bar Seven bunkhouse as cowboys, brandishing guns and hastily dressed, went plunging through the chill in search of the trouble.

Dave knew none of this, nor did he know that a full-bodied girl was standing on the veranda of the owner's house, her wrapper held in numb fingers, horror and hope, alike mingled in the large blue eyes that watched the lamps bounce as the riders fanned out, searching for the victim of the shooting and praying it wasn't her lover.

Chapter Five

WAR

Dick smoked in saturnine silence, clearing the crevices of his teeth from the remnants of breakfast with the point of his tongue. Dave looked awful, across the office from him. The bandage and its purple cargo that showed around it were sickening enough, but his hollow-eyed, whisker-stubbled face made the whole picture worse. He listened grimly.

"That's two, Dick. Jerry Turk had it coming. This Josh—I don't even know."

Dick shrugged. "Seen him around, but didn't know him. Anyway—he's a damned fool for getting mixed up in it. Self-defense, both times, though. You got no worry there."

"Not there, I agree," Dave said dryly.

Dick grinned harshly. "No, not there is right. I got a hunch Murdock and George'll move fast now. They got to. By their lights they got reason to kill you now. They'll try like hell to get it done today. Things like this don't ever lag much. They can't. Folks get to thinking, then they don't like the idea of a big outfit gunning a lone man. Even a squatter."

Dave got up, shot a glance at the pale light outside and shuffled his feet uneasily. "Well—I got to keep moving.

That bushwhacker makes me think I dassen't head back to the meadows. Arrowhead's got me moving eastward and I've got to keep going that way. By now they know what happened to their stake-out at Bar Seven."

"Yeah," Dick said, spitting into his palm and snuffing out the cigarette. "They're pushing ahead of 'em like the In'yuns used to do the buffalo. Figure directly they'll have you flushed out into the open, like here, in town, maybe, then they can finish it quick." He nodded to himself. "Here—I made up this complaint after I got back from Arrowhead. You got to sign it before it's any good."

Dave regarded the paper doubtfully. "What good'll that do?"

"Plenty. I got authorization, then, to round-up George and Murdock and jail 'em. Attempted murder, trespassing, and even destruction of private property. I threw that last in just for the hell of it. I don't know whether it'll help any or not, but it won't hurt any."

Dave was shaking his head. "Can't do it, Dick. I owe George something. If you lock him up, I can't get my payment."

The deputy hacked lustily and spat towards a brass spittoon. "Listen, Dave, you'll get your licks through the law. That's the best way. Hell—you go out hunting George and I'll wind up being a pallbearer again." He was shaking his head. "Besides—like I told you on the meadows, I'm in this on your side. Just give me a couple of licks at those Arrowhead renegades and so help me, I'll fix every spoke in their wheels, legally, for a long, long time."

"I appreciate that, Dick, really, but let's wait a while on this complaint. At least until tonight."

Newton sat back looking at Dave. He read the finality in the rider's eyes and bit back his flare of temper with an effort. "All right. We'll do it your way, then. But I'll be out with the warrant for both of them right at sundown. Now sign the damned thing so I can make it legal when I go after 'em."

Dave signed, bending over Newton's desk. The deputy made another cigarette and somewhere, a long way off, a rooster squawked his defiance of the new day in Danville. Dave reversed the paper and shoved it towards Dick.

"I got your word on it, Dick. Don't go after 'em until sundown."

"That's right." He lit and inhaled. "Now tell me something. Why in God's name would a man like Roy Murdock risk everything he's got to fight a down-at-the-heels ex-cowboy? It don't make sense to me."

Dave shook his head. "He's like Lester—and the others. They've faced every challenge the same way. With guns. The Mesa's changing, but the old-timers don't change with it."

Dick spat again. "Goddamned poor reason to risk your ranch and your life, if you ask me?"

"Me too, but these mossbacks think differently, Dick. They've been the law too long. They go all-out even in small arguments—and you know that."

"All right. You're right and I know it. Knew it when I asked. But it still don't make sense. Not to me." He looked up. "Now what you got in mind? Not going to

70

sail over to Arrowhead and take 'em all on, I hope."

Dave shrugged and smiled wryly. "No. I can't go back. Murdock'll have Arrowhead guns waiting for me on the meadow. He'll likewise have 'em stashed out around Bar Seven and, for that matter, all over the damned Mesa."

"Maybe in Danville, too."

Dave nodded. "Maybe."

"Well?"

"I'm going to have the doc check this bandage. It's pretty dirty." Dave was grinning at the deputy, "And you can go to hell for the rest of the information, old bronco. I know what you've got in mind and I don't need any wet-nurse."

Newton looked a little startled for a second, then he burst into a shrill, uncontrolled laugh and wagged his head. "Goddamn—you're pretty coyote at that." The laughter ended but the look of humor, and appreciation that Dave had read in his mind lingered. "All right, have it your way. A pony of rye says they'll kill you before sundown."

Dave nodded slowly. "All right. I'll take it. Only—if you win, you'll lose, because I won't be able to pay up. Besides—if they get me, your warrant'll be that much stronger."

Dick leaned back in his chair and shook his head. "Nope. You're forgetting something. I'm also custodian of corpses as well as deputy sheriff. Coroner. I'll get the cost of the pony out of your wallet, or peddle your guns for the cost." He waved a skinny hand. "You're lucky in a way, though. I've made that same damned bet a hundred times, I reckon, and only once have I collected on it."

Dave eyed the new day with a faint smile. "All right, Sheriff. You might as well be my heir anyway. I got no other—except—Lucy." He moved towards the door, opened it and grinned back. "Adios."

Dick Newton was out of his chair in a flash. He crossed the room towards the door snatching up a sawed-off shotgun as he went, threw the panel wide and stood in the doorway watching Dave Reed cross the deserted roadway towards the doctor's place. There wasn't a sign of life in the town yet. It was too early.

When Dave disappeared beyond the doctor's front door, the deputy eased off the hammers of the riot gun, stood it in a corner and went outside again, walking leisurely down the duckboards towards the livery barn at the extreme north end of Danville, eyes brilliantly cold and searching. He knew the finale was in the making. Experience told him that, and he intended to be in on the final act.

"Well," the doctor was squinting at the flesh under the bandage and working with hands that operated independently of his mind. Trained, thinking hands; the kind every good doctor has. "It didn't hurt much before because it was partly numb. This time you'll cuss."

"How's it look?" Dave was asking automatic questions. The pain was negligible, now, and he was thinking of Arrowhead, not his wound.

"Oh—a little worse. They always do." The hands were cleaning the flesh and working regardless of the patient's suffering.

72

Dave had to grind his teeth twice before the new bandage was being made up and put on. "How's the face going to look?"

"Well—sort of early to say, with any certainty, but I'd guess you'll have a scar about four inches long and maybe a half-inch wide, over your cheek-bone. There'll be—dammit hold still—these little black specks of course. They're powder burns. Mostly, they show up worst during the winter when a man's skin gets lighter."

"How about the ear?"

"That's something else again. Ever see a fish-hook ear mark on a critter?"

"Sure." Dave felt like grinning at the doctor's bluntness. "About like that?"

"Kind of. I had to trim off the hanging meat, y'see. Trim the thing up and dress it so's it wouldn't look too damned bad. Well—it'll look presentable considering the big rip it had from that big piece of lead. You'll have this fish-hook ear mark all right."

Dave spoke his thoughts dryly, half humorously. "I'm glad it isn't an undercrop and dock like Arrowhead uses."

The doctor said nothing for a second. He seemed to be pondering whether he should say anything or not, then he risked it. "One of the Arrowhead men do this to you?" Dave nodded, smelling the odor of strong pipe tobacco as the man worked on him.

"I'm a poor man to give advice," the doctor ventured. "It's never any good anyway, but if I was to advise you, young feller, I'd say sign a complaint against Arrowhead; let the law handle them for you and crawl into bed and give this thing a chance to heal for a week or so."

"Can't do it."

"No," the doctor's voice had a mild lacing of irritation in it. "I suppose not. Got to ride over the country trying to get an infection in this thing that'll kill you slower but just as sure as any Arrowhead bullet'll do. You fellows are all the same."

Dave felt the strong, pudgy hands drop away from his face, linger for a second on his shoulders as the medical man leaned back and studied his bandaging efforts then leave him altogether. He looked questioningly at the doctor, who was fishing in a shapeless coat pocket for a pipe, regarding him shrewdly.

"What do I owe you this time?"

"The same. Three dollars."

Dave paid him with a tiny frown. "Costs as much to get bandaged in Danville as it does to get fixed up in the first place."

The doctor looked over his pipe bowl at him with sardonic blue eyes. "Well—the first time the thing looked so bad I forgot to charge you full price. Besides—it's harder for me to make a bandage than it is to carve off a leg. There's no such thing as a nurse in Danville." He puffed contentedly and scratched his fat ribs deliciously. "Now I got to travel to Bar Seven and that'll kill the day for me." He pocketed the silver dollars and failed to see Dave's swift look.

"You taking care of Lucy Mallow?"

The doctor got up nodding, looking past Dave's eyes at the thick bandage again. He answered absently. "Yes, she's got the measles—Spanish measles. Pretty old for 'em, at that." His eyes gradually came back to Dave's glance and saw the interest there. "Why? You know her?"

"We're going to be married. That's what this is all about."

"What?"

"I homesteaded Mesa Meadows so's we'd have a ranch of our own and a home."

"The hell." The doctor removed the pipe and squinted at Dave. "I knew you'd homesteaded up there. It's common knowledge." He cleared his throat. "So you're the hombre Lucy was crying about when I first went out to see her." He looked closer at Dave and began to shake his head gently. "Well—I don't know. Seems to me she could've done better." He was grinning wryly and Dave liked the twinkle in his eyes. They both laughed.

Dave explored the bandage with his right hand, was agreeably surprised to find that it was smaller than the other one. "Will you take a note to her for me?"

"Sure. There's no charge for that." The doctor fished inside his coat for a pencil and some blank paper. "Make it up next time I bandage you anyway."

Dave wrote swiftly, folded the paper and handed it back with the pencil, scooped up his dusty hat and nodded. "Gracias, Doc. See you again."

He was half out the door when he heard the doctor's dry reply. "I wouldn't be the least bit surprised if you did."

Danville was reluctantly coming to life, facing another hell-hot midsummer day. People were stirring

75

here and there but the hitchrail before Colton's Saloon was vacant. Dave knew it would be, for an hour or two, maybe more. He started down the duckboards towards the place, sensing rather than actually seeing, the startled looks of the few passers-by as he walked.

The bartender—he of the handsome auburn moustache—looked around over one shoulder when Dave's spurs rang softly across the deserted room. The man was setting up bottles on a back-bar shelf and froze that way, his eyes starting from his head.

Dave grinned crookedly at him and recalled the man's sentiments towards homesteaders as made evident the last time they had talked.

He asked for ale before he saw the sign, evidently made by a hand more guided by wrath than erudition, to one side of the bar. NO DAMNED CLOD-HOPPERS SERVED AT COLTON'S BAR. His eyes came back slowly to the bartender. "Make it two ales, pardner."

The bartender didn't hesitate. Wooden-faced, he drew them both and set them up, took Dave's money and was moving away.

"Here—one of these is for you. Drink it."

The bartender looked over at the bandage, the dark, stubbled face with the hostile, ironic eyes, came back and reached for an ale with a shrug.

"Colton didn't put that sign up. It was one of them riders. Young punk."

Dave drank off the ale and set the glass down. "You had many Arrowhead riders in here, lately?"

"Oh, about the usual number," the man said carefully.

"Last night?"

"Yeah. Some last night." The barman finished the ale, put both glasses under the bar and made a graceful swoop with one hand, backwards, under his moustache.

"George Marsters?"

"Uh—no. I don't recollect seeing George in here last night. Night before he was in. Him and old Murdock, together. First time I ever seen Murdock come in with his riders."

Dave nodded absently. "You still hate homesteaders?"

"Never did hate 'em. It's just that I'm around folks who do all the time. I got nothing personal against nesters. It's nothing personal."

Dave watched the beads of sweat rise up unevenly on the man's forehead and smiled. "I'm not pushing you, pardner. I came in for a drink, not a fight."

The barman's eyes looked grateful, but his face was still ashen and taut with fright. He levered up a weak, asinine little smile and nodded at Dave. "You got quite a face there."

"Yeah. Haven't I? I owe that to George—to Arrowhead."

"That so?" The voice lacked timbre, seemed to want nothing so much as to end the conversation forever.

"Yeah. It was four to one. Pretty big odds, and I lost out."

Dave knew the man had heard of his shooting down of Jerry Turk. He guessed that Arrowhead's version was far from the truth. "I paid 'em back partly, though. Two of the riders who were in on it, are dead. Jerry Turk was one of them. The other was the 'breed they called Josh. Got him before dawn this morning out at Bar Seven."

He watched the shock spread behind the auburn moustache and smiled wolfishly. "All homesteaders aren't clod-hoppers, you know."

"Sure not," the bartender agreed. He didn't sound convinced though, and he wasn't. A strong thought was running through his head. What Arrowhead would do to this man when they caught him. He had no doubt they would. One squatter against six or eight of the hardest riders and fastest guns in the Mesa—fatal odds. He raised his eyes slowly and regarded Dave impassively. It was hard not to feel pity for the man. The bandaged face with its swollen, purplish flesh, his lean, gaunt look, and his obvious courage. He shrugged. "Listen, pardner. Don't hang around in Danville too long. It ain't safe for you."

Dave finished his ale and nodded soberly. "I reckon it isn't." He looked up at the seven-point buck over the backbar and admired the animal's aloofness once more, then nodded to the barman and walked out of the saloon.

Danville was bustling now. Dave crossed through the traffic of horsemen and light buggies and made the opposite plankwalk. He knew, by the way people looked at him, that news of his presence in town had spread fast. He was passing a beefy man with an unnaturally tight string-tie and heard the man gasp when he was still a half a foot in front of him. The man's eyes were looking towards the north end of town. Dave knew the hefty man, all right. He ran the saddle and harness shop. Slowly Dave stopped and looked back. His own shock was even greater than the harness-shop man's.

78

George Marsters was threading his way through the stunned traffic with a lifeless body lashed to a horse behind him. Dave recognized the corpse. It was the 'breed.

Danville made room for the Arrowhead foreman, who rode directly towards the deputy sheriff's office, grim-jawed and cold-eyed. Dave stepped into a convenient store, which turned out to be a Mexican café, and watched George go by.

"I can help you, Senor?"

Dave turned, studied the ingratiating smile on the fat, greasy face and nodded as he swung low on the bench before the plank counter.

"Yeah. I reckon. *Huevos y tostados.*"

"No *carne,* Senor? *Puerco?*"

"All right. Ham or bacon with it. Got coffee?"

"*Seguro.* I'll get that first."

Dave drank the coffee and thought. It was time for a recapitulation. He sensed the critical stage of his battle as being current. Success or failure were balancing on the narrow bench with him. Without knowing exactly how this was, he nevertheless sensed it being so, and turned the affair of homesteading Mesa Meadows over in his mind without another thought of George or the 'breed, whom, he knew instinctively, were with Dick Newton right then. Up to that point, Dave's reasoning was good, but here it veered off and became personal, as it should, and here destiny took a hand, as she always does, and sent an informant to George with the news that Dave was in Danville. Absolutely ignorant of the new turn of affairs, Dave relived his entire life as it had

79

been for the last forty-eight hours, and pondered it well for a key to the future.

Fate, though, had already cast her shadow before Dave Reed. While he thought of his trouble, George Marsters listened grimly to the fact that the renegade cowboy was in town and kept the knowledge to himself, avoiding the chance that Dick Newton might object to primitive plans of vengeance, and also harboring a suspicion, in common with Roy Murdock and the rest of the Arrowhead, that the deputy was a little less than neutral, after the way he had reacted to Jerry Turk's death at the ranch headquarters.

"You're sure?" George's dark face was intent on the man.

"Yes. Sure as hell. Seen him just a few minutes before you rode into town."

"Where?"

"Well—he was down the road a piece. About where the surveyor's office is. Next to that greaser café."

"Thanks, pardner." George didn't smile or look especially thankful, but the informant accepted the cold thanks and left. A trickle of reproach was already dampening his enthusiasm for a good gunfight and killing. He headed through the dust for the saloon, justifying his despicable behavior desperately and weakly—and without success of any kind.

Dick Newton joined George on the duckboards in front of his office. He regarded the Arrowhead foreman with veiled dislike. "Well—it may be like you say. I'll investigate. If he was shot down in cold blood, there'll be trouble, but tell me one thing—what in hell was an

Arrowhead man doing, hiding out in the brush near Bar Seven headquarters about four in the morning?"

George was caught off balance. He wasn't smart enough to fabricate on the spur of the moment. Always before, that had been Roy Murdock's end of things. He made a small, angry gesture with his hand. "Chriz'. We don't keep night-herd on our riders. Maybe he was coming back from town. I don't know. Anyway, that's got nothing to do with shooting a man down in . . ."

"No?" Dick asked dryly. "Maybe not, George, but this man was shot down from the front. His six-gun's unfired, like you showed me, but I also notice his saddleboot there is empty. Where's the carbine?"

George's mind was floundering, so he took refuge in anger. "Damn you, Newton. Arrowhead's not going to stand for none of your . . ."

"That's enough, Marsters. Plenty. I've got the power to slam you into jail for a damned long time. Got it signed and ready in my pocket. Just one thing keeps me from doing it. My word. Now listen and take this back to Murdock. Arrowhead's making one bad play after another in this mess. You're heading for a peck of trouble and you'd better slack off. That's a warning, George, and I mean every goddamned word of it. So far you've broken three good laws." Dick held up a hand and raised a finger each time he spoke. His right hand was conveniently close to one gun butt. "Attempted murder. Trespassing. Willful destruction of private property. If that's not enough, I can dig up more."

Newton let his hand drop to his side and his eyes didn't waver from the heavier man's face. "I don't believe this story about the 'breed either." He didn't say he already had Dave's version and that it matched perfectly with what he had observed on the dead man. The leaf mould on his levis, the bullet hole in his forehead and the vanished carbine, plus his presence in hiding at Bar Seven.

"You better pass this along to Murdock. He's getting in deeper every minute. I'm giving you fair warning, and it's final. Stay off Mesa Meadows and don't mess with Dave Reed. I'm talking law, George, and I'm not kidding one damned bit."

George's features were wooden all through Dick's harangue. He didn't move. Inwardly, he was exulting. A certain slyness kept him calm. He knew about where Dave was and intended to kill him, then race back to Arrowhead. Roy Murdock would take care of the rest of it. He'd said so, before the hands, when news of the 'breed's killing had come back to them.

George's face was as deliberately stony as were his words. "Then you ain't going after Reed?"

Dick shook his head shortly. "No. Not to arrest him. If Murdock wants to come in and sign a complaint, I'll pick him up and bind him over. A court of law can decide the thing then."

George left without letting any of his elation show. "All right, Dick. All right." He turned and headed down the duckboards, spurs ringing sullenly and his thick body rolling with each step.

Dick watched him go with a puzzled look. A small, wondering frown. It had been too easy. George Marsters had something on his mind. The deputy shrugged,

82

fished for his tobacco sack, felt the signed warrants in his pocket and darted an appraising glance at the sun. Sundown was still a long way off. He made the cigarette and lighted it with impatience, then went over, loosened the cinch on the dead man's horse and led him down the road towards the livery barn. The few clotted spots of blood on the saddle were hosting frenzied, glistening blue-tailed flies.

Chapter Six

PURSUIT

Dave finished eating, paid the Mexican and left the café. His horse was tied to a fence on the west side of town, so he cut into a back alley and started down through the refuse, feeling better than he had in many hours, still wondering whether he dared go back to Bar Seven to see Lucy. He needed someone to talk to, to help him plan strategy, and thought of her as the logical one. A man looked out at him from a tarpaper shanty, narrowed his eyes and stood motionless in thought, then raised his head and called out.

"Hey—Reed."

Dave turned, recognized the man as a sometime round-up hand used on Bar Seven in rush seasons and raised his eyebrows, waiting. "Yeah?"

"George's walking the town for you. Just seen him cross the road down by the livery barn. The word's gone out. You'd better get to horse."

There was no scorn in the last words. The rider was no

more a hero—or a fool—than the next man. Prudence and common sense were all that contributed to longevity on the frontier. The rash men died young and were buried deep.

Dave hesitated. In his case there was a difference. George was the secondary cog in the destruction that was hurtling towards him. Also, there was the personal grudge over his being shot in the face and disfigured, nearly killed, while unable to defend himself. He nodded soberly. "Thanks, pardner. I'm glad to know it." The man at the door of the shack watched him reverse his course and stride down the alley towards the north of town. There was a bitter glint of savage excitement in his sunken eyes.

Dave's senses went into a sort of automatic transition to wariness and stealth. Danville had two gunmen stalking one another, like apparitions, through the heat of the day. It didn't take long for people to understand what was in the making. It was a sort of frontier sixth-sense. People who lived with death and face it every day of their lives, developed an intuition about it that was uncanny. Such an aura of alertness descended on the cow-town now. Word of mouth passed the bare minimum facts from person to person and gradually the main roadway emptied itself of all but the extremely curious and the foolhardy. The aim and decision to shoot, of men risking their lives is rarely dependable. Danville crawled into its shell, waiting for the storm to pass over.

Dave made the rear maw of the livery barn easily and stepped into the gloom, redolent and strong with an odor of hay, ammonia and horse sweat, but his quarry wasn't there. He went up the wide, raked down earthen passageway and grinned at an old man, a hostler, who was watching him.

"See any Arrowhead men lately, Dad?"

The hostler nodded once, brusquely. "George's on the other side of the road. He crossed over not more'n five minutes ago. Listen—boy, you'd better get Dick Newton. He's the fastest man with a gun in these parts. You can't . . ."

"All right, old-timer; all right. Thanks." Dave saw the interest turn into rebuff on the man's face and he grinned again, moving in close to the front wall before he peered up and down the road. Three or four clumps of men were standing close to strategic openings between buildings, talking earnestly and squinting over the town, but George wasn't in sight. He hesitated to cross the open roadway, looked around and saw the old hostler harnessing a solid looking chestnut buggy horse.

"Bring the horse over here, pardner." The man did, with a quizzical look. Dave motioned with his gun to the road. "Just lead him across the road. Stay on the left side of him and I'll be right behind you."

The hostler's eyes widened in understanding. His eyes swept frantically from Dave's gun to his eyes. Neither offered any compromise. The man spat a thin, amber stream, gave Dave a look of anger and scorn, turned back and hiked out of the barn on the left side of the chestnut. Dave followed, made it to the opposite side of the duckboards and darted between two buildings to safety. He had a brief glimpse of the hostler turning the horse and going back to the barn. Some vivid cuss words drifted to him and he smiled in understanding before pushing on down the littered little pathway and emerging in the alley, where he swung south and began his march up through Danville again, towards Colton's Saloon.

But George didn't materialize. The alley was deserted except for huge rats and an occasional tomcat, unless one counted the alarming hosts of flies. Dave traveled the complete length of town and came out again at the upper end, where he came around on to the duckboards again and stood, unmoving, letting his eyes rake over everything that was moving, or still and two-legged.

There wasn't a sign of George. People were stirring again, timidly. The sidewalks were carrying a trickle of humanity that had assumed one, or perhaps both, of the combatants, had ridden out of town.

Dave shrugged and started down towards the heart of town. He passed Newton's office on the opposite side of the road and gradually came down by the sooty opening to the blacksmith's shop, and then he saw George. Across the road, his back to the traffic, in conversation with two Arrowhead riders who were close to the hitchrail where they had just tied their horses after riding into town. Dave could see the riders' faces. They looked predatory and intent. He smiled to himself. George would be telling them of his plan to kill Dave Reed. Maybe even detailing them to aid him in the search of the wanted man. Dave pulled his hat low and kept the pedestrian traffic between himself and the roadway where the saddle and buggy traffic went blissfully about its business, completely unaware that it served as an efficient screen for Dave's use in getting closer to his prey.

Only the road separated them, when Dave slowed, stopped, and leaned against a handy upright post that supported the overhang in front of Colton's Saloon. He saw a large ranch wagon approaching and made his move quickly. As soon as the big, lumbering supply outfit was close, he stepped into the dirt of the roadway and started towards the Arrowhead men. He was close, having timed it so, when the wagon ground by. Three more steps and he was close enough to see the weather-lines in George's neck. Then he spoke and saw the two pair of eyes widen in horror as the Arrowhead riders, facing him, got a jolt of recognition.

"One move, George, and you're dead. Just one move. You there." Dave's gun barrel tilted towards the rider. "Take his guns and let 'em drop."

The man's frantic eyes looked into George's face. The foreman knew the voice. He wasn't moving. Slowly, stiffly, the rider disarmed George. There were specta-tors, too, but again the word had gone out and people were disappearing from the sidewalks again, or staying a long way off, watching.

Dave nodded curtly. "Now yours. Do it left-handed, boys. Just let 'em drop. Fine. Back up. Over against the building." The riders obeyed, stony-faced.

"George—turn around and move out into the road. Farther. Good." Dave stopped, gathered the guns and tossed them overhand one at a time. They could hear the dull, heavy sounds as the weapons landed on the store roof, overhead, then Dave holstered his own gun and started towards the Arrowhead foreman. Some startled townsmen, astonished, came closer and made gruff, garrulous sounds.

George heard Dave speaking as he came in, but didn't pay much attention. He was vastly relieved that the traitor was going to seek his vengeance with his fists. George was easily forty pounds heavier and six inches taller. He relaxed and balled his fists, flashing the unarmed Arrowhead riders a triumphant, ironic smile.

"Let's see how you make out without guns and riders to back you up, George."

"Hell—you're a damned fool, Dave. I'll kill you this time. You got guts, I ain't denying you that, but you're a damned fool."

Dave rushed in, stopped and feinted. George swung a mighty arm that missed by ten inches. He swore, conscious of the growing crowd and the ripple of soft noise that swept among the spectators, when he missed with his first blow. Then Dave flashed outward with a probing that drew George's attention, crossed over with a stinging right that connected high on the foreman's chest, and went in fast, under a killing barrage of lefts and rights and slammed two hard, jolting blows into George's stomach. The Arrowhead man's great size seemed to wilt a little when the sour taste of bile tinctured the saliva of his mouth and he gasped through clenched teeth.

Men in the crowd were crying profane encouragement to Dave. George's teeth parted enough for a vivid string of blasphemy, then he began a slow march towards Dave, who stepped back and away, sideways, watching the dark, contorted face before him.

George's strategy was simple. Force Dave to stand by backing him into the crowd, then pummel him to helplessness. It was the age-old tactic of brute force and brute intelligence.

Dave backed into the fringe of the crowd, set himself, legs spread, and watched. George roared and bore in fast. Dave timed it with fright in his throat, then, at the last minute, he dropped to one knee, twisting sideways, and drove his right fist like a battering ram, into George's midriff. For a brief second he could feel the warmth of the man's belly through his shirt touch him high on the wrist, then the big body went backwards a little and he looked up. George's arms were hanging at his sides. His eyes were bulging and glassy. Dave came up fast, driving his fist upwards with the momentum of his upward spring. The knuckles slammed into George's jaw, under the left ear, with a sound like a small caliber gun. Still the Arrowhead foreman didn't go down. He weaved and staggered, but instinct kept him upright.

Dave took two steps forward, lashed with a left that rocked the larger man backwards, then fired a murderous right into George's battered stomach that bent the foreman over. The men were stamping their feet and howling like wolves when Dave swung one arm like it was an axe and clubbed George Marsters at the base of the skull and stepped sideways as the great bulk went forward on knees that finally refused to support the numb bulk any longer.

Dave watched George fall. He went forward gracefully, unconscious and relaxed and struck full force, face downward, in the dark, moist spot where a horse had been tied, and slid for a foot before he stopped and lay still. There was a lacing of blood on his cheek where the jar of the fall had whipped it backwards from his torn mouth. He seemed to flatten and widen as he lay there.

Dave turned to the crowd. A squat, incredibly muscled-up man in a filthy undershirt and wearing a slick, dark leather apron, was shouting above the furor and waving at the two Arrowhead riders still standing back against the saddle-shop wall. He looked over, saw nothing to alarm him and pushed through the spectators and headed once more for his horse. George hadn't touched him once. The air being sucked into his lungs felt like sulphur and his muscles twitched, but he exulted inwardly over his victory. It was premature exultation, but Dave didn't know it.

He got his horse, swung up and reined around westward. The need to see Lucy was stronger than ever now. The great breadth of land before him on all sides and ahead, riding slowly through the shimmering heat, he could look up into the purple distance and see the proud, upward life of Mesa Meadows far off. His ranch. Their ranch. Then there was the sound of running horses. He turned, surprised at riders who would ride hard in such killing heat and saw four men coming pell-mell down the land after him. Alarm was telegraphed to the horse. Arrowhead riders coming from the direction of Danville!

Dave lifted his horse into a lope, cursing at the twist of fate that put these men behind him, and grimly satisfied that, whoever they were, George Marsters wouldn't be with them.

Riding only fast enough to keep his lead, he figured the Arrowhead riders must have ridden into Danville shortly after the defeat of their foreman, and now were running him down for vengeance. He vaguely recalled someone saying something—maybe it was George—about Roy Murdock offering a cash reward for him, dead. Twisting in the saddle, he looked back. Nothing but such an incentive could make the riders thunder after him like that.

One man rode erect, his looped reins swaying wildly. He pulled out his carbine and levered off a shot. Dave's horse added another notch of speed in sudden terror at the sound. The rider, his bandaged face glistening with greasy sweat, palmed his six-gun and held it ready. He knew there was little danger from the rifleman, but the men were closing in. Dave swore and squinted at their horses. The animals were ringing wet and running automatically. He studied the land around him. Ahead, a mile or so, was a willow-fringed creek. In the clear atmosphere of the shade, over there, he could distinguish tail lashing cattle standing in the coolness fighting their endless battle with heel-flies.

The fight for life, to Dave's mind, was going to be a comparison of horseflesh. His was still fresh and strong, but he wanted to conserve that might, too, in order to reach the creek. In order to do that, he had to let the Arrowhead men gain a little, then, feeling they were close enough, he hunched forward and closed his knees gently against the rosaderos. The horse went willingly lower, belly down and ears back, towards the rapidly looming-up thicket. Dave took a long look at the alerted cattle who were trotting off, high-headed, watching, then he looked back towards his pursuers.

The reckless rider with the unlimbered carbine shot again and levered up his third shell, looking over the lowered rifle towards Dave.

Two of the other Arrowhead men flashed their six-guns in glittering arcs and shot high. Dave made a grimace at their foolishness and reined quickly in among the willows, leaped off his horse in a running sprawl and let the horse go. It roared on through the thicket, scaring out cattle in every direction, crossed the stingy little creek and thundered on, head high, tail erect and reins flopping wildly.

"Come on out, Reed."

Dave pressed closer to the ground, feeling its coolness through his clothing. The smell of cattle, strong and pungent, was all around him, along with bands of aroused little heel-flies. He smiled bitterly to himself, searching for a target. A pair of horses' legs went by his hiding place, but he didn't fire.

"Reed—we'll kill you if you stay in there. Toss out your gun and come on out."

Dave's scorn overcame his prudence. He swore at them loudly, moving deeper into the bush as he did so. "Come on in and get me, Arrowhead. You'll get worse'n George got. George, Jerry and the 'breed. What'm I worth—dead or alive?"

The same reckless voiced man yelled back at him. Dave guessed the speaker to be the carbine-wielding cowboy. "A thousand dollars either way. Don't be dumb. Come out unarmed and you'll go back to Murdock astride. Keep on horsing around, damn you, and you'll go back tied sideways." The man punctuated his promise with another random shot with the rifle.

Dave heard the slug ripping overhead. Twigs fell close by. He edged backwards until he was lying in the creek itself. Here, the smell of cattle was stronger. Their sign was everywhere. He lay still and listened. The spokesman didn't fool him any. He knew the man was talking—trying to hold his attention—while the others crept in where they might get a shot at him.

The flies were bad and then mosquitoes came, too. Dave cursed them under his breath and listened for the slightest sound. When it came, he knew no fly or mosquito made it. It was the soft song of a spur rowel caressed by a twig, to his left and ahead. Without waiting, he snapped off a shot and the answering challenge came right back and threw tepid water and mud on him. Angered, he fired twice more and edged forward in the slime. No more shots came from the unseen killer, but a fusillade of gunfire erupted on his right; three hand-guns and a carbine.

Dave put his head down and waited for the furor to cease. He was consumed with irrational hatred for the spokesman with the carbine.

"Reed—damn you—you got five seconds to say you're coming out—then we're coming in after you."

"Go—to—hell!" Dave spaced the words carefully,

so that their enunciation would carry clearly, then he turned completely around and began crawling rapidly down the creek as best he could, without making a lot of noise. It wasn't hard so long as he stayed in the water itself, but the fallen leaves and dry twigs on each side of the bank were eager to betray him by their closeness.

The Arrowhead riders started relentlessly into the willow fringe, making no effort to keep their location a secret. Dimly Dave could hear them swearing at the whipping willow branches. He continued his retreat making as much speed as he dared, then, suddenly, he was in a shallow spot where generations of summering cattle had killed the brush on both sides and left a bare spot six or eight feet wide. Here, Dave studied the country on both sides of him, saw nothing but drowsy, tail-switching horses of the Arrowhead on his left side and squirmed out of the creek on to the parched, sere ground where he lay flat and relaxed for a long moment catching his breath and resting.

The pursuit was floundering profanely in the near distance. Dave could hear them. The strident voice of the man he recognized as the spokesman, came clearly down-wind to him.

"I'll add a hundred to Murdock's thousand. Damn his soul for getting us into this—anyway."

Someone grumbled back at him. "I'll give you a hundred to flush him out of this damned swamp."

"Dammit! I don't believe he went up creek at all. Look-a-here. There. Them's tracks of some kind. I'll bet the damned snake went down-creek."

Dave ground his teeth and forced himself to his knees. His body was achingly tired and he felt a tangible hatred for the man with the carbine, and his raucous, nagging voice. He eyed the Arrowhead horses covetously and got to his feet slowly, testing himself all over, then sprinted recklessly towards the horses. He circled them cautiously, slowed to an ambling walk and caught the reins of an inquiring grulla gelding, swung into the saddle and swung the romal at the remaining animals, let out a wild yell and hazed the animals farther west, across the creek and over Bar Seven. An anguished shout and some wrathful gunshots shattered the thick heat waves behind him. Dave rode until he found his own horse, caught the animal and turned the Arrowhead mounts loose. Bewildered, the riderless horses watched him ride way towards Bar Seven. One started to follow, hesitated, then went back to its fellows and all four of them dropped their heads and grazed indifferently. The four walking specks bearing down on them angrily, and leaving a swath of livid profanity riding the still air as they came, went unnoticed by the horses, and Dave too, as he loped easily towards the buildings that were growing larger as he went down the range.

Bar Seven wasn't deserted when Dave rode in. Lester Mallow was standing, hip-shot, leaning on a pole corral with one of his riders. They were guessing gross weights on some fat steers penned within. One rider turned at the sound of a loping horse, looked startled and nudged Lester. The big rancher turned slowly, ponderously, and watched Dave rein to a stop and swing

95

down. He wasn't as surprised as one might think, from looking at him. The rider eased his back against the corral and looked impassively at his ex-riding companion, turned nester. There wasn't enmity in his face but there wasn't any great cordiality either.

Dave nodded, walking towards the men. Lester turned to the cowboy and spoke under his breath shortly. The rider looked disappointed, shrugged and turned away, moving slowly and reluctantly. Lester eyed Dave blankly until they weren't more than ten feet apart, then he spoke.

"Well—you've got guts, showing up here."

Dave looked closely at the big man's face, read nothing there and shrugged. "No choice. There're four Arrowhead riders behind me."

"What'm I supposed to do? Help you hide?"

Dave flushed. "No, not exactly. I'd like to trade you my horse for a fresh one. Don't like to kill a good horse just because some bronco bucks are behind me."

Lester didn't answer right away. He was looking dispassionately at the bandage. "Four of 'em? That's pretty big odds, isn't it?"

"Not a matter of choice, Lester. How about that horse. I can't stay here talking all day."

Lester nodded slowly, shoved off the corral and started for the big barn. Dave fell in beside him. They were in the wide doorway where a cool, horsy fragrance enveloped them, when the ominous thunder of running horses made both stop and turn. The Arrowhead men were riding headlong into the yard. Lester's practical eye took in the condition of the horses and his eyes flared briefly. The riders saw Dave and rode in close, drawing their guns as they came. Lester's indignation catapulted him forward in the face of the furious cowboys.

"What in hell do you mean, charging into Bar Seven with guns in your hands?"

The nearest rider, a wizened, pock-faced man spoke coldly and Dave recognized the voice. It was the spokesman back at the creek. The man with the carbine, only now he had a six-gun in his right fist, balancing the thing cocked, like a club.

"We want him." The gun tipped towards Dave.

Lester spread his massive legs. Indignation showed in every line of his body. "Put those guns up. No one comes busting into my yard like that." He jerked his head sideways without taking his eyes off the Arrowhead riders. "This man's on Bar Seven property and no one bothers him while he's here."

One of the Arrowhead cowboys swore angrily, leaning forward in the saddle. "Listen, you. We don't . . ."

"Shut your damned mouth!" Lester's wrath made him look twice as big. "Turn those horses around and get to hell off this ranch. Now!"

The wizened man's eyes flamed. The gun barrel came down slowly, but Dave had anticipated it. His own gun was out and arcing upward, but a new voice interrupted the tension. It came from in front of the bunkhouse. Three Bar Seven riders were standing there. Two with carbines, one with a brace of handguns. One of them swore coldly. Dave recognized the voice. It was greying Jim Yarbro, oldest employee of

Lester Mallow. A dyed-in-the-wool Bar Seven man.

"Go ahead, bronco. Jest let that thing go off. By gawd you'll be the second one dead."

There was a thick silence. The flushed faces swung towards the bunkhouse, saw the array of defiance, and the horsemen lost a lot of their confidence. The odds were changed drastically now, instead of being four to one, or two, it was now five to four. The wizened man in the forefront of the Arrowhead men seemed to hesitate. Dave felt the wavering decision and spoke up.

"Go on. Ride off. You're trespassing here, just like you did at the meadows. Go back and tell Murdock that. Vamoose!"

There was no other choice. The Arrowhead men, once so close to the reward offered for Dave Reed, turned reluctantly and filed out of the Bar Seven yard. Once, the wizened man twisted backwards in the saddle and glared at them, but he said nothing, turned back straight again and rode on towards Danville.

Lester nodded approvingly at his riders. "All right, boys. That's enough. You can forget it now."

Yarbro snorted. "I wouldn't bet you even money on that. Not with Roy Murdock and George Marsters behind 'em. Nossir, and that's a fact."

Lester didn't reply. He faced Dave thoughtfully. "Come on around to the office." Dave followed the big cowman and dropped thankfully on to the bench while Lester went around his old desk and eased into the squeaking swivel chair.

"Well—dammit. Looks like I'm in it." Lester's eyes were baleful.

Dave scowled. "No, not necessarily. If you'll let me have a fresh horse, I'll ride on."

Lester grunted and squirmed in the chair, shaking his head. "No." He spoke slowly. "It was about to come to this, anyway."

"What do you mean?"

"Well—there was a cattlemen's meeting the day after you moved up on the meadows. Murdock called it. We met in Danville." Dave nodded. He remembered Lester's absence from Bar Seven the day he had first told Lucy about homesteading Mesa Meadows.

"It was pretty noisy. Roy and some others were for getting you off one way or another. I was against it. There weren't many against Murdock's plan, though." The big shoulders rose and fell. "But it split the association, anyway, and that's all I wanted."

A shadow darkened the doorway. Both men swung their heads with instinctive alarm. It was Lucy, dressed in faded, tight levis and a cotton shirt of blue and white checks that swelled around the abundance of her breasts. She looked at her father inquiringly, then let her glance wander over to Dave. She looked astonished and horrified—and Dave remembered the drying mud and slime on his clothes from crawling down the creek.

"Dave! What've you been . . . ?"

"Come in, Lucy, and sit down." Lester addressed his daughter in the same slow, deliberate tone he had been using to Dave. The girl came in, went over and sat next to Dave, taking his hand. Dave noticed the way her mass of tawny hair was held at the base of her neck with a green ribbon, then Lester was talking again, looking dourly at them both.

"Listen, Dave. I fired you for a reason. Two reasons. I'm not blind, boy. I knew how you and Lucy have felt towards each other. Boy, she's all I've got. I'd see how things were with her, any time. Always have."

Lucy spoke then, interrupting. "You wanted to split us up—is that it?"

Lester shook his head vehemently. "No, not at all. You misunderstand, honey. You're too young. I wanted Dave Reed to grow up. Quit being a cowboy and grow into a rancher. There's a whale of a lot of difference. I wanted to force him into doing what he should've done five years ago. Strike out on his own. Not be a damned rider all his life." Lester slapped the desk top open handed. "I wanted him to use his head instead of his rear, to make a living with. Dammit, Lucy, I didn't want you marrying someone's hired hand. Do you see?"

Dave's small frown persisted. "What made you think I couldn't just ride on, Lester?"

The rancher growled deep in his throat. "I didn't know, Dave. I gambled, that's all. In the first place, you'd been acting restless lately. I figured you were beginning to think about the future a little. That's the way it struck me, when I was younger than you are. And in the second place, I figured Lucy had too much of a hold on you for you to ride on." He leaned forward in the chair, looking at them. "But I'll be damned if I expected you to dare and homestead Mesa Meadows. That was a hell of a shock, boy."

100

"Lester—you and Murdock don't really need the meadows. You've got more land than you need as it . . ."

"I know that. That's exactly what I told the association. That Arrowhead and Bar Seven alone have access to that land and both of us can do without it, therefore the other cowmen had no right in the mess at all. Some went along with me. Others sided with Murdock."

"Well," Dave said simply, feeling greatly relieved that he wasn't going to have to fight Lucy's father after all, and also beginning to have an inkling why Bar Seven hadn't molested him on the meadows. "I'm obliged to you, Lester."

"Obliged my neck," Lester said tartly. "You owe Lucy a lot, boy. Not me. Now then, Murdock's not going to let this thing die where it is. I know him too well to expect that. He's like iron. All the old-timers are like that. Running his riders on Bar Seven has put me against him out and out. He'll see it that way, some day."

Lucy's eyes showed affection for her father although her face wore no expression at all, unless it was a tincture of tension.

"Dad, I thought that was it. Mother and I both did, when you wouldn't talk about Dave. You didn't side with him openly or join in fighting him either. I'm grateful too, Dad."

"Well," Lester was obviously uncomfortable under his daughter's praise, "forget that kind of talk. I just wanted him to be a man, and you to marry one—if you're going to."

"I am, Dad." Lucy said it simply and squeezed Dave's filthy hand. He returned the pressure without looking away from Lester. Also, he felt the back of his neck getting turkey-red.

"All right." He was at a loss to say more. Lucy's two words had shaken him badly. He had known, of course, that she wouldn't stay at Bar Seven forever, still . . .

"Lester, you don't have to side with me. It's going to make you a herd of enemies. I've got the law on my side, anyway. My right to Mesa . . ."

"Dave—in cow country there's no law going to favor a nester over cowmen. Don't you ever forget it. Not until there are more voting squatters than there are cattlemen. Maybe then things'll change. I don't know." He scratched his ribs before he spoke again. "I've lived longer than you have, boy. You've started a war to the finish with Murdock and he'll fight you just that way, don't make any mistakes there. Old Roy's a fighter through and through. I'm in it, now, too, so there's just one thing left to do. Fight."

Dave shoved off the bench and stood up. Lucy clung to his hand but remained seated looking from her lover to her father, saying nothing.

"All right, if you won't sit back, then let's ride, but I sure feel funny about having Bar Seven riding with me against Arrowhead."

Lester arose slowly with a hard shine to his eyes. "I'm sorry I've got to buck Murdock. Hell—we've been friends for close to twenty-five years, but the old devil won't listen. Time's are changing, boy. Not just on the meadows and in Danville, but all over the West. Those that are too blind to change with 'em, will go under. All right—that's off my chest—now what's this ride talk about, anyway?"

"I'm going to Mesa Meadows."

"Dave!" Lucy got up and stood looking into his face. "That's crazy. There's nothing up there any more. You said so yourself. What do you want to go up there for?"

"Lester—if you'll ride to Danville and get Dick Newton and bring him back to the meadows, maybe we can end this thing."

Lucy didn't give her father a chance to speak. "I'll ask you again, Dave. Why?"

He looked down at her. "Because I'm going on to Arrowhead. I'll need a hostage. One Arrowhead man."

She was shaking her head at him. "No, honey, please. Wait for Dick. Don't go to Arrowhead. Murdock'll . . ."

"No, not if I've got a man of his in front of me, he won't. I want to talk to him. If he won't listen to reason, then I'm going to bring him back to Mesa Meadows. He'll assure me of getting off Arrowhead alive, just like his guard on the meadows will get me through to him."

Lester was pondering the idea thoughtfully. "It's crazy, Dave. Roy'll never go back with you. Not even if you use a gun on him. He's not that kind. I see why you want Dick and me on the meadow, though . . . so's you'll be able to wind the mess up where it started . . . on your ground."

"Right, Lester. Will you go after Dick?"

Lester shook his head. "Nope. But I'll send a couple of the boys. Jim Yarbro and I'll ride to the meadows with you. Don't fool yourself, Dave, you'll need us before this day is over."

Lucy's hold on Dave's arm was tight and afraid. She tried to think of something to say, couldn't, saw no compromise in his face, bit down hard on her lip and turned away, going out of the office with sight blurred by tears. She went around the house in search of her mother.

Chapter Seven

MESA MEADOWS

Mesa Meadows stretched away before the three men like a matted carpeting of dryness intersected by the small, rushing creek that bisected it from the waterfall farther back in the pine forest westward. Jim Yarbro's slitted eyes flashed over the wreckage of the bunkhouse and shook his head gently.

"Lot of work gone to hell."

Lester nodded without speaking. According to Dave's plan they were to stop by the wreckage and stay there, in plain sight. Lester wasn't surprised when a solitary horseman came out of the forest and rode towards them. He grunted softly at Yarbro.

"He's got a carbine across his lap."

Yarbro nodded brusquely. "Yeah, that's a fact. I can see the reflection from here."

"You know him, Jim?"

"No. Don't recognize him. Not yet anyway. It's sure as hell not Dave, though."

"No," Lester said. "Dave said he cut into the trees from the south trail, over by Arrowhead and come in behind anyone who's hiding out back there. I reckon he's behind this rider now."

Yarbro nodded again. "Hope so. This guy's got the gun handier'n ours."

The Arrowhead man stopped several feet away and looked at them both for a long second before speaking, then he nodded towards Lester Mallow, whom he recognized. "You boys looking for someone up here?"

"Yeah," Lester said gently. "Dave Reed."

The cowboy snorted wryly. "You won't find him back here. Last I heard he was in Danville. Word came to the ranch he was, early this morning. George went in before we knew. Roy sent in four of the boys, though, afterward." The man's hand relaxed on the carbine. It was evident by his bearing that he was tired of his lonesome vigil. "You're Lester Mallow, aren't you?"

Lester nodded. "Yeah. Where's Murdock?"

"At the ranch, I reckon. You want to see him?"

"Not particularly," Lester said. "But I expect I will before the day's over."

Yarbro saw Dave coming across the land behind the Arrowhead rider and made loose conversation as long as he could to keep the man's attention facing forward, then, when he knew the cowboy was between two fires, he shrugged and jutted his chin.

"Well, Arrowhead, you're way off. Miles off, in fact."

"What're you talking about?" The man's hazel eyes tightened on the carbine.

Lester raised his hand and pointed behind him. "Dave

Reed's behind you, hombre, about two-hundred feet."
He watched the violent start the man gave and lowered
his head a little. "Don't be a damned fool, feller. You'd
go to hell two ways. Let the carbine drop easy and nothing'll happen."

The cowboy's face paled. He stared rigidly ahead at
Lester and Jim. The sound of Dave's walking horse was
plain in his ears, like muffled drumming.

Lester wasn't smiling. "All right. It's your choice.
Drop it or use it. Two in front of you and one in back.
Poor odds but make your play."

The Arrowhead man let the carbine slip away. Lester
waved Dave forward. He came slowly, warily, reached
over and disarmed the rider and reined up beside him,
looking over at him. There was a small, cruel smile
around his mouth. A thin strip of white, compressed
flesh showed above the upper lip. He nodded.

"What's your name, hombre?"

"Bradshaw. Terry Bradshaw."

"Terry, turn your horse and ride for the Arrowhead.
Don't make any faults, Terry, and nothin'll happen."

Bradshaw didn't. He turned and rode slowly, sullenly,
back towards his home ranch. His eyes were bitter out
of the dark flush of his face but he was no fool either.

The trail was still under the high-noon sunblast. The
four of them rode carefully, letting Yarbro ride ahead of
Bradshaw, while Dave rode behind him and Lester
brought up the rear, uncomfortable on his horse and
wincing from the unaccustomed punishment he was
taking.

The Arrowhead buildings were ghostly quiet as the

men rode into the yard. Dave swung down, keeping his horse between himself and the main house and motioned the others to dismount.

"Lester—you and Jim stay here. I'll take this hombre with me. If Roy's in there . . ."

"No," Lester said fiercely. "I'm in this too." He turned to Yarbro. "Jim watch our stock." He gave the rider no chance to argue, but turned away and went along with Dave behind Bradshaw, who was looking at the house anxiously.

They were almost to the veranda when a door opened ahead and Roy Murdock stepped out, a carbine hanging easily from his hands. "All right," he said flatly. "That's far enough. Plenty far. Bradshaw—step to one side." The cowboy needed no second command. He moved swiftly and easily, and stopped to the right of Dave. Murdock's hard eyes went over Lester Mallow with a scathing glare. "Lester—you finally out in the open with this—clod-hopper?"

Mallow nodded. "Like I told you at the meeting, Roy. You're making a bad showing for the rest of the cowmen."

"Hell," Murdock shot back with blistering scorn in every word. "It's you that's made the damned fool of yourself. You recollect how most of the boys backed me up?"

"Sure, but it was the minority of smart ranchers that didn't Roy. Think back—there was Cliff Given and Tenn Birch and . . ."

"To hell with them, and you too. You're backing this whelp because you'll have the meadows for Mallow stock. Don't you suppose we know Reed's going to marry Lucy?" The carbine barrel swung up a trifle. "I just figured it out, myself, a few hours ago. The reason you didn't want to buy in and protect the early feed on the turn-out, is because you'll get it anyway if Reed makes his squatting stick." Murdock swore then, savagely and unstintingly and Lester Mallow reddened visibly. "Well damned if you'll get the meadows for Bar Seven, I'll promise you that."

"I don't want it, Roy. Now or in the future. I don't need that land any more'n you do. You're being pigheaded, that's all. Pig-headed and damned foolish. Dave's trying to make a home for him and a wife, is all. If any Bar Seven cattle get up there in the future, I'll be paying head-right fees on 'em, just like I would on any leased land."

Murdock's glance flickered to Dave. His thin mouth was drawn down harshly. "You've got guts, Reed, riding back here after last night."

Dave turned. "It doesn't take guts for a man to go home."

"Home," Murdock snorted. "You never had a home."

"Maybe not like yours, but that log house you blew up was home to me, just like the meadows are. So far you've tried force to get me off, now I'm here to try arbitration. You call it quits and so will I."

Murdock laughed his sarcasm. "When I quit, Reed, it'll be because you're under the ground. I told you before, go somewhere else and squat. Anywhere in the Mesa country but on these meadows, and Arrowhead won't bother you. There'll be no arbitration as long as you're on Mesa Meadows, and especially after you shot down two of my riders."

Dave nodded slightly towards the carbine. "You're the one that started this war, Murdock, when you sent George up to my place to run me off. Jerry Turk got what he bargained for. So did your 'breed. George, too."

Murdock's eyes widened. "George? Where's George?"

"I left him lying in the road in Danville."

The rancher's face went slack-jawed in astonishment. He had received no word concerning his foreman since George rode off to take the dead body to town. Dave took advantage of the man's surprise to yank his gun. The barrel pointed directly at Roy Murdock's belt buckle.

"Drop it!"

Murdock's eyes were stricken. He saw something ominous staring up at him for the first time in a long life. Defeat. Complete and utter defeat, and by a single man, at that. The carbine fell at his feet and his stricken look passed from Dave to Lester. He nodded slightly. "You helped him, too, Lester."

Mallow shook his head. "Not with George I didn't, Roy. This is the first I've heard of that fight."

"Well . . ."

"No. You know damned well I've stayed out of this thing up till now. I wouldn't be in it now, either, if four of your riders hadn't come charging into my yard loaded for bear, guns out and spoiling for trouble." Lester's massive shoulders rose and fell. He and Roy Murdock had never been close, but they had always got

109

along. They were a lot alike; too much so to be intimate friends. Lester felt sorry for his neighbor, in a way. "I kept neutral because I wanted to see Dave, here, prove himself. It's different when Arrowhead riders come busting into Bar Seven looking for trouble. I make that my business, Roy."

Murdock said nothing. His hard eyes flickered from one to the other. "All right, Reed, what's on your mind?"

Dave walked forward without answering, relieved Murdock of his sidearm and gave him a gentle shove off the gallery of the house. "Head over there by the horses."

They took the back-trail through the forest towards the meadows. No one spoke until they cleared the fringe of trees and came out on to the curled down carpeting of dry grass, then Jim Yarbro squinted ahead and grunted.

"Looks like the boys found Newton, all right. He's over there, and that's a fact."

Dave looked. There were three horsemen lounging by his shattered log house. He smiled thinly when he recognized Dick.

Newton rolled a cigarette with jerky movements, his lean, angular frame erect by his horse's head, watching the four riders rein up nearby. He nodded, lit the quirley and eyed Murdock with obvious distaste.

"Well—Roy. You had enough?"

Murdock's glance was bitter. "You'll find out, as soon as I get a lawyer out of Glenwood."

Dave swung down, holstered his gun and studied the

110

two Bar Seven riders. They were still sitting their horses, regarding him with wonder and speculation. He knew them both and nodded. They nodded back in silence.

Dave turned to Dick, glancing at the sun on the horizon, where it was sinking rapidly towards a notch in the far-away hills. "I reckon you could cheat a little, Dick. It still lacks an hour or so to sunset, but I imagine that'll be overlooked."

Deputy Newton nodded thoughtfully with a hint of humor in his eyes. "Yeah. Yeah I reckon you're right at that. I could cheat a little." His eyes went to Murdock as he extracted a limp paper from his pocket. "Roy Murdock—you're under arrest."

Murdock's face tensed. He started to say something, seemed to think it over, then gritted his teeth together until his jaw muscles bulged dangerously.

Dick was watching his prisoner closely. "Attempted murder," he intoned dully, "trespassing, destroying private property, disturbing the peace, obstructing justice and . . ." Dick looked up again. "Hell—a lot of other things that I haven't filled in yet."

Dave wanted to laugh but the gravity of Murdock's face and the unhappy look of Lester and his riders kept him from making a sound. He shook the sweat off his nose irritably. "Well—let's get back to town, Dave. If we horse around too long, George and those other Arrowhead riders might show up and make things awkward."

Murdock's head swung around swiftly. He glared at Dave. "I thought you said you killed George?"

111

"Nope. All I said was that I'd left him lying in the road, at Danville. Didn't say anything about shooting him. Matter of fact, I fought him with my hands, not guns."

Murdock's look changed abruptly. He flashed a fast appraisal at Dave Reed's body, looking for the secret of his victory over George Marsters, bigger, heavier, and supposedly tougher than the homesteading cowboy. He shook his head, doubting, and turned back forward in his saddle as Lester rode in close and gigged Murdock's horse with a boot-toe.

"Come on, Roy; ride along."

They rode slowly across Mesa Meadows, took the wide trail to the undulating lowlands and swung southwest across Bar Seven. Lester sent his two riders to the ranch with instructions to inform Anne and Lucy that he'd be late in getting home.

Newton rode beside his prisoner, silent like the others. When they got to Danville the town was alive with speculation. Somehow the magic story of their coming had preceded them via the mysterious range grapevine. Men watched them ride by, stony-faced. The town felt like Dick Newton; in favor of the underdog. But the range men, the ranchers, riders, and cowmen, were for the most part solidly behind Roy Murdock.

Dick Newton swung down before his office and tied up. The others followed suit. They crossed the duckboards and went into the small building, Roy Murdock's face getting harder, more flinty with each step that brought him closer to the final humiliation of a jail cell. Inside, it was gloomy with the late afternoon shadows. Dick Newton reached overhead for the lamp, to light it, when a harsh, deep voice spoke into the gloom and froze him the way he was standing, hands high over his head.

"Steady. Don't move, any of you. Roy—get their guns."

Dave saw George before the others did. He sucked in his breath shortly. The Arrowhead foreman wasn't alone. The same four riders that had pursued him to Bar Seven were coming out of the dark corners, guns up and menacing.

"George, you're making a fool play. Arrowhead can't buck the law, no matter what Murdock says."

George squinted at Dave wrathfully, then swung his swarthy features towards Murdock. "Any orders, Roy?"

Murdock stepped clear of the others nodding his head. "Yeah. Just like you're doin'. Disarm 'em." It was done easily by the Arrowhead riders. Murdock's triumphant smile was tight and brutal. He nodded again at George. "Good man, George. Good man. Now, by gawd, we'll end this thing. Get some rope, one of you boys."

"A lariat all right?" someone asked.

Murdock smiled again, harshly. "Just right. Get it."

Dick Newton was watching them over his shoulder. "Murdock—you're a damned fool. Resisting the law'll break you, sure as God made green apples. No damned cowman on earth is that big. I'm warning you, Murdock. Put up those guns and . . ."

"Thanks," Murdock said, as the rider handed him a coiled lariat. He ignored the deputy except to tell him to put his hands down and faced Dave. "You're coming with me. So far, you've had plenty of luck, hombre." He waved the lariat in Dave's face. "Let's see how you'll squirm out of this!"

Murdock's meaning was clear. A hanging for the man who had come so close to beating him in the fight for Mesa Meadows.

Lester Mallow's baleful eyes widened with amazement. "Roy! Have you lost your mind, man? Good God—you're making yourself a murderer—an outlaw—and over land you don't need. Don't be a complete damned fool."

Dave knew Lester's words were wasted as he listened. He was watching Murdock's face, read the resolution and unflinching determination there, and shook his head. "Lynching me'll only put you in so deep, Murdock, you'll never climb out. Sure, I'll lose Mesa Meadows, but you'll lose a damned sight more. You'll lose the meadows as much as I will and probably your Arrowhead spread."

"Yeah," Dick Newton said dryly, "and more'n likely your life as well. That rope trick works both ways, Murdock."

"The hell it does," Murdock said sarcastically, eyeing Newton with open distaste. "Well—you're partly responsible too, lawman. You've sided with this damned renegade right from the start. I've seen to it that Sheriff Stanley hears about it. Any time the law won't do it's duty, then the cowmen will." He turned to Mallow with a savage jerk of his head. "I ought to take you along, too, Lester. You're as much a traitor as Reed, here."

Lester's eyes showed scorn. His voice echoed with the contempt he felt. "Go ahead, Roy. You'd probably like to, all right. But man, you're not all there upstairs. You're crazy loco; you must be, to do a thing like this and not think of the consequences."

Murdock nodded shortly. "I've thought of 'em, all right, Lester. I can show justification for everything I've done so far. Don't forget Jerry Turk was killed while still on Arrowhead land, and the 'breed was shot down from ambush on Bar Seven, which is—or should've been—neutral land. And then this fool and you kidnapped me off Arrowhead and turned me over to your cohort at Mesa Meadows." Murdock's head was wagging back and forth. "I've thought of a lot of things, Lester, and by God I think I can explain every Arrowhead action up to now."

"That so?" Dick said, acidly. "And just how in the devil will you explain this lynching bee, Murdock? That's been against the law, regardless of circumstances, for quite a number of years."

Murdock was actually smiling. "There won't be a lynching, Newton. I'm no fool." He poked a gun at Dave. "Walk, hombre, out the door and over to the hitchrail. Fault me, boy, and I'll blow your backbone out. Move!"

Dave moved. He threw searching looks at Lester, Dick Newton and the two wooden-faced Bar Seven riders as he went out of the office past them. On the plankwalk, only George, Roy Murdock and one Arrowhead rider were with him. Murdock holstered his gun, swung up and reached for Dave's reins.

"Get up, Reed."

George nodded to the rider beside him as they mounted. "Stay here, Clem. When we've been gone a half an hour or so, tell the boys to head for the ranch and stay there. Don't let none of them fellers inside get loose for at least a half an hour, otherwise they'll foller us."

Murdock nodded at the cowboy, who looked disappointed that he wasn't included in Dave Reed's lynch-party, and nodded glumly as the three horsemen rode slowly down through Danville, where the setting, blood-red sun was sinking behind the far off mountains.

Dave's empty holster rode uselessly on his hip. He speculated on making a lunge for George's gun, or Murdock's, but knew it was hopeless. Stonily, he went along, between them at a distance they both maintained—out of reach.

Near the south end of town, Murdock swung northwestward. Dave was surprised. He had assumed that Murdock would take him to the meadow, or at least to Arrowhead, before he hanged him. That the rancher rode towards the rolling land north of Danville made him frown. Lester and Dick wouldn't expect the kidnappers to take this route, either. Dave looked over at Murdock, saw the savage set of the man's craggy face and looked away. Roy Murdock was a murderous man, which came as a surprise to Dave. He knew Murdock's reputation for hardness, but he had never had occasion to suspect its vindictive, deadly depths before.

Suddenly Murdock held up his hand. They all stopped. George was looking at his employer with a puzzled frown puckering his dark, broad forehead.

"Someone coming. Rider."

Dave heard the soft, slow sound of horse's hooves then, too. He leaned forward hopefully.

George swore angrily. "Let's get into the brush."

"No." That was all the time Murdock had. The stranger loomed up out of the shadows of dusk. All three recognized him immediately, and Roy spoke shortly, in answer to the other man's careless, hand waved greeting. "Evening, Doctor. Out kind of late, aren't you?"

The doctor reined up his gentle, lazy old mare, almost as fat and out of shape as he was. The twinkling blue eyes whipped over the men rapidly, then came to rest on Roy Murdock's face. He sighed and slouched with a head shake.

"No. A doctor's got no regular hours. That's the price he pays for his calling, Mister Murdock." The blue eyes saw Dave's empty shell-belt holster, raised them slightly to his face and read the urgency there.

Murdock was frowning. "Well, we've got a long ride ahead of us."

"Sure, I expect you have. I'd like to have another look at that face, though, first, if you don't mind." The doctor's horse went in close beside Dave's animal. George shot a glance at Roy Murdock, who shrugged irritably and watched the doctor's hands flick upwards, lift the bandage a little and probe.

Dave held perfectly still. He felt the slight tug of a

117

small, added weight in his empty holster and guessed the medical man had dropped a derringer into the thing. A quick look at Murdock and his foreman showed nothing but annoyance on their faces. Dave relaxed although the dull thunder of his pounding heart was loud in his ears.

"Well—as good as can be expected, I suppose," the doctor said. He turned and shook his head at Roy Murdock. "It's a bad one, though. Well, good night, gentlemen. See you again." He lifted his reins and shot Dave a close look with a calculated wink in it. "Oh—Dave. I forgot to tell you. I gave Lucy your note. You and Lester had ridden off just before I got there. She's as good as new, son."

Dave nodded, puzzled. All he had said in the note was that he loved her and would see her that night—which he wouldn't be able to do now, and probably never again. "Thanks, Doc. I'm obliged."

"You're welcome. She said she'd ride over to Arrowhead and wait for you. Good night."

Dave looked after the slouched rider, but the doctor didn't look back. He was just a sound in the darkness when Murdock, staring at Dave, reined in beside him. "Now, just what in hell did he mean? We aren't going to Arrowhead."

George began to swear lustily. "Hang the dirty whelp right here, Roy."

Murdock's edgy temper flared at the foreman. "Shut up! You think I'm stupid enough to hang him—after what Newton and the others know? Not by a damned sight."

Dave looked from one man to the other, more puzzled than ever. If Murdock wasn't going to lynch him, then what was he going to do?

George's dark face grew sullen. "Well—what'd you bring that lariat for, then?"

"For looks, you fool. Reed's going to get hit over the head and have his foot shoved through the stirrup . . ."

George's face cleared. "Oh, I'll be damned. That's better yet. That hanging had me worried a little, I don't mind telling you." He laughed softly. "The old drug to death alibi." His smile included Dave affably. "Best there is. Lord only knows how many riders've been taken care of that way."

Murdock was ignoring his foreman. His baleful glance was fastened on Dave. "All right. What did the doc mean about the Mallow girl waiting for you at Arrowhead headquarters? Spit it out!"

Dave had been thinking fast. He knew the doctor had been trying to give him, if not a stay of execution, at least a temporary reprieve. He gave Murdock stare for stare. "Well—I told her you and I'd be over there, at your place."

Murdock smiled dourly. "Good. She'll be traveling in the opposite direction from the way we're going."

Chapter Eight

DEFEAT

George Marsters was taking it all in with a descending frown on his hard, dark face. He looked to Murdock for an answer to Reed's words. None came. Murdock was sitting stiffly erect in his saddle looking at his prisoner.

George grunted uneasily. "Listen, Roy. There's a lot here I don't like." He had the distinct sensation that a noose was being lowered over his head. He shook himself unconsciously.

Murdock unbent a little. Some of the stiffness left him, but the hard look didn't. "Reed, you're not smart enough to out-guess me. You've had a lot of luck. A whole damned pot full."

Dave shrugged. "What about your four riders back at Danville?"

"Yeah," George said. "What about 'em, Roy?"

"Shut up, George. Just listen, don't think." The rancher's eyes raced back to Dave. "All right. Maybe you're right. Right or wrong I'm not going to take any chances. We can't horse around with you any longer." The brittle eyes flashed at George. "Shove his foot through the stirrup." While he was still speaking, Roy Murdock kneed his horse in close, drew his gun and raised it, watching Dave like a starving wolf. George slid from the saddle, tore a spur off Dave's right foot and wedged his foot through the ox-bow stirrup with no little pain to the homesteader.

Dave saw the gun descending and timed it. When the breadth of the thing was within inches of the crown of his hat he lunged forward and hooked the startled horse with one spur. The animal exploded under the murderous cut of steel, but not quite quick enough. Dave's fingers were clawing wildly at the derringer in his holster when the rancher's gun struck him at the juncture of the shoulders and the neck with blinding force and giant pinwheels went off just behind his eyes.

Someone shouted as Dave's horse raced away. It was George. He had his gun out and swinging to bear on the wobbly shadows disappearing into the night.

"You didn't hit him hard enough, Roy, damn it."

A gun exploded once, twice, then, after a lull, a third time.

Roy Murdock saw Dave going sideways out of the saddle and smiled bitterly, raising a hand at George. "Hold it, you fool, the doc might still be close enough to hear."

"Well—Jeezuz!" George exploded vehemently. "You didn't get him."

"The hell I didn't. He was going off just before he went out of sight."

George looked back into the night, saw nothing and heard only the very faint drumming of a running horse, and swung back at Murdock hopefully. "You sure?"

"Hell, yes," Roy answered. "Come on. We got to be at the ranch when Newton shows up. He'll arrest us sure as hell, but no law on earth'll let him hold us. He'll never prove we killed Reed."

They rode off in a long lope, southwest, towards the

distant range of Arrowhead, both thinking differently on the same subject, Dave Reed.

Dave's mind was frantically tearing at the shroud of unconsciousness that seemed to be rolling inexorably out of the back of his head, numbing the senses as it came. His right hand went for the saddlehorn, missed it, went back for another wild grab that partially succeeded. The thunder of shots added to the nightmare, with its blanketing numbness that came on. He knew the saddlehorn was under his hand but couldn't make his fingers close around it. He was slipping sideways, could feel it and was helpless to stop it. The horse raced out of control. Each lurch sent him farther to the left, out of the saddle. It was the frightened urging of frantic instincts that finally overcame the numbness enough for him to force both arms up, quickly, for the horse's mane. He missed again and fell back.

The agony of a wrenched leg shot through him as he struck the ground. It acted like ice water. The pain and the terror both. Dave's eyes flashed wide. His hand went to the holster again as the thought processes shook free of their lethargy and told him to kill the horse. He was feeling for the small gun when something dark snaked across his face and cut with its momentum. He reached up and yanked at it and the horse slowed a little, head high, turning inward, to the left towards the dragging burden.

Dave forgot the derringer and reached for the rein again and tooled the badly frightened animal to an uneasy stop. He lay there, feeling the horse's fright transmitted through his outstretched leg. The animal was quaking. Dave didn't move for a while. The pain from his ankle made him sick inside, and he had a prodigious headache from Murdock's blow. Slowly, forcing himself to do it, he sat up, waited until the dizziness left and reached for the tie-strings dangling from the rear saddle skirt, and pulled. The effort made his body break into a clammy sweat, then he was standing beside the horse, watching its ears.

The animal stood bunched, nostrils dilating in discomfort and his ears quivering back and forth in uncertainty. Dave's words flowed over him in a soft, easy, sing-song tone and that alone held him steady.

A finger flicked the cinch, found it snug, and Dave summoned his strength, reached for the mane and horn and vaulted back into the saddle using only his right leg for the spring up. The horse snorted a little, then Dave was astride, where he should be, and the animal relaxed.

It had been a harrowing few minutes. Both Dave and the horse let the tautness go out of them slowly, thankfully, then he reined around and headed for Arrowhead.

He was past Bar Seven, south-west, before he coaxed the little under-and-over derringer out of his holster. There was a wry smile on his face as he looked at the little thing lying in his hard palm. The doctor had had no choice, but a six-gun holster was probably the worst place he could have dropped the thing. It had slid far down and wedged there. Dave broke it, saw the two large caliber shells one over the other, snapped it closed again and stuck it into his pants pocket.

He stopped not far from Arrowhead, reached far forward and tugged at his boot. Surprisingly, it came off in spite of the swollen ankle. Withdrawing his foot back through the stirrup, he put the boot back on, dismounted gingerly, tied the horse among the Digger pines that fringed the north-east area of Arrowhead's ranch yard, and hobbled on afoot.

There were no lights and a certain formidable eeriness hung over the ghostly outlines in the weak moonlight of the gaunt old buildings, solemn and ghostly.

Dave stood in black shadow, studying the yard. A wift of tobacco odor came to him, but he couldn't locate the red end of the quirley itself, try as he might, but there was satisfaction in knowing his prey was on the ranch, close by, probably sitting in the darkness waiting for visitors, guns ready.

Studying each building carefully, Dave slithered through the night. He was behind the blacksmith shop, coming down across the yard in complete darkness, when he saw the form loom up ahead, moving away from him, hunched over. Thinking it was either George or Murdock, he limped rapidly forward and swung his fist in an overhead arc that bowled the other man forward on his face. Kneeling, Dave clinched it with a murderous slug to the jaw. The man was limp when his face rolled upwards and Dave looked at him in surprise. It was one of the four Arrowhead riders who had held the deputy and Lester Mallow and Jim Yarbro, at gun's point back in Newton's office. Dave took the man's gun and examined it. Fully loaded, it was an old weapon and scarred, but Dave was satisfied. He regarded the unconscious man with wonder. There was nothing to tie him with, so he arose and stepped over the body, hugging the back of the blacksmith shed and wondering how many men were in hiding, waiting, at the Arrowhead. The four riders, George and Murdock made six. Dave smiled thinly to himself. They were waiting for the law to arrive, apparently, and weren't expecting Dave Reed, at all. Least of all, Murdock and George. If he could find those two, he could easily control the cowboys.

Dave decided, then, as long as Murdock wasn't doing anything but waiting, he'd go back by the old barn and wait too. Newton was sure to bring reinforcements, a posse, and no man in his right mind would go up against odds like faced him, on Arrowhead, alone.

Engrossed with these thoughts, Dave had almost obtained his objective, hobbling carefully through the gloom, when a man's form materialized at the side of the barn, where no one had been before. Dave saw him and dropped low. The big, bulky shadow straightened warily. The voice that came huskily out of the night was familiar. Dave gripped his gun tighter, tilting the barrel upward, belly-high.

"That you Marsh? Say—goddammit—straighten up. What's eating you anyway, it's me, George. Don't be so nervous."

Dave's ankle was shooting pains up one side into his head. He knelt on one knee, looking at George. "This isn't your rider, George," he said evenly, "this is Reed, the hombre you left dangling from a stirrup."

Dave could hear the sharply indrawn breath, then George swore wildly, making no move towards his guns. He didn't dare. The watery, dark light reflected off

125

the .45 pointed at his stomach. "Jeezuz! Dave . . ." He said no more. There wasn't anything to say.

Dave's upper lip had that ridge of white above it. He nodded slightly, eyes wide and deadly. "Yeah, Dave. George—I owe you this. You and your boss, both. You're first."

George used the sound of Dave's voice. He had no way to even it up, but he swept into action while Dave talked, gaining a five second respite. It was close, at that. George Marsters was no novice. He got off one shot that was close. His second stabbed into the ground at his feet. A geyser of powder-fine dust erupted.

Dave fired the first time where he was holding the gun. He saw George take it, too, and rock back against the barn wall, then he raised the gun a little and shot again. George didn't appear any worse and Dave thumbed off two more fast ones and pushed himself upright, watching the Arrowhead foreman sinking stubbornly, reluctantly, fighting every inch of the way, to hold himself upright, the way he had in Danville, then he crumpled and sagged forward like an old blanket, and lay still.

Dave went over to him even when he heard the shouts in the yard, over by the house, and toed him over to make sure George Marsters was dead. His sightless eyes, still moist, shone like moonstones in the sickening moonlight. Dave un-cocked the gun, holstered it and moved off, limping, listening to the voices around him coming towards the scene of the fight slowly.

"Roy—it's over there. Beside the barn."

"George? Where in the hell are you? Answer up."

Someone found the body, Dave lay flat in the fringe of Digger pines, watching. Another Arrowhead hand edged up by the first. They both glared at the body, then one of them swore with ardor and glared around the yard. Roy Murdock and another rider came up. No one said anything for a moment, then Murdock raised his head with a puzzled, startled look on his face that Dave couldn't see, but his voice telegraphed how he felt.

"George! Go'almighty."

One of the three riders looked at the others. "Where's Ernie?" No one said anything for a while, then Murdock looked from one rider to another. There was consternation in each face. And fear of the unknown that seemed inherent in the nightly stillness.

"Lesten. There's something going on around here. Who'd shoot George like that. You boys see anything?"

"No," a nasal, rasping voice that Dave recognized as the man who had hunted him with the carbine said. "Not seen a damned thing. Where'd you reckon Ernie went? We ought to look around. Maybe he got shot, too, in this scuffle."

Murdock's angry voice interrupted. "Like hell. Forget Ernie. He'll turn up. There's some son-of-a-bitch on the ranch getting us. We got to get him first."

"Yeah. Might be that damned deputy."

Murdock swore at the rider. "He don't have to bush-whack. Besides, he'll have men with him, I expect, and that's what we've been listening for. No, whoever this hombre is, he's slipped in on us."

A droll, calm voice with a Missouri twang to it spoke up then. "Well, if somebody done slipped up on us, I just don't believe it's no stranger. Not by a damned sight."

Roy faced the man. "What do you mean?"

"That I didn't hear no rider coming, and I'll lay you money that killer's right here, amongst us." There was a shocked silence, then the ironic voice went on. "Don't ask me his reason. I don't know it. But we've all been sitting around here. No horseman's going to slip up on us, 'thout someone hearing him, I don't think."

Roy Murdock said nothing. He was looking at the man as though he had never seen him before, then he nodded his head slightly. It had to be something like that, then. He only had one enemy who had the guts to tackle Arrowhead on their home ground, and that man was a long, spidery-intestined, sickening red ruin behind an exhausted, run-out horse somewhere. And Newton—he wasn't the type to fight this way. When he came, there'd be horse-thunder to announce him, and he'd ride in erect in the saddle. Murdock looked back at the dead man saying nothing. Wondering.

Dave had no idea of the thoughts of the three men he was watching. It was puzzling, too, the way they acted. He had the gun cocked and aligned on them. He wanted Roy Murdock and the pock-marked man with the objectionable voice, but he didn't want them quite this way; not outlined dimly against the old barn, accessible for murder.

The Missouri twang spoke up again. Dave heard the words plainly, this time, because the others were perfectly still by George's body.

"Well—where is Marsh?" No one answered. The

Missourian answered himself. "I'll lay you odds he's sloped. He ain't around here and there's been no other gunfire. He ain't been downed, by Chriz'. Then where is he? Gone—the buzzard. He's the one. Must be. It don't make sense but what else is a man to think?"

Roy Murdock was gripped by a sudden and complete knowledge of his own defeat, and with it, came the unpalatable realization that, in the fight for which wasn't really his in the first place, he had jeopardized everything he owned and his life as well, and now this murderous dissension in Arrowhead ranks itself, was overwhelming him. He shuffled slightly and his spurs made soft music in the stillness. Somewhere, down the line, he had made a bad mistake. A calculated error of tremendous proportions, and it struck him dumb. He looked from one rider to another saying nothing. The cowboys sensed his feelings easily, even the weak pale light from the sky showed the shattered strength and doubt that lay, like a whiplash, across his hard features.

Dave watched in complete fascination. He understood that, somehow, the Arrowhead was breaking up. He couldn't know it was from within, thick with suspicion and fear, that the riders and their leader were being demoralized and bewildered. All he knew and cared was that Arrowhead was cracking up and he, one lone homesteader, had contributed immeasurably to the ruin and defeat of the second largest cow outfit in the Mesa country.

Slowly Dave raised himself, confident that the risk wasn't nearly as great as it appeared. He knelt on his sound leg, favoring the swollen, sore one, and tilted his head back so that his words would carry across the shadow world to the unsure, shaken men standing by George's corpse.

"Murdock. Don't a one of you make a move. Put your hands on top of your heads and don't bat an eye."

For a second none of the four men moved. They were thunderstruck. The Missouri-voice swore grumpily and obeyed the command slowly. All of the men, except Roy Murdock. He recognized the voice and was horrified by its presence.

"You, too, Murdock. Put 'em up there or full 'em!"

Murdock's mind reeled off the things this enemy before him could impale him over, legally, and still he made no move.

"Goddammit, Roy," the pock-faced rider, who was standing close to the Arrowhead owner said, "do like he says. You want to get us all killed?"

Roy's hands went up as though his body ached and each motion was agony. His eyes were wild with hatred; unreasoning, primitive wrath, the kind that destroys everything around it, and the one who possesses it, as well.

Dave stood up, then, and faced them. His triumph was pleasant, in spite of the soreness of his body and the near-fever in his head. He started forward to disarm his prisoners, and that alone saved his life. A rifle exploded in the night, not far from the blacksmith shop but closer to the bunkhouse, and the night went to pieces in a tumult of wild yells and gunfire.

Dave didn't have time for swearing, even. He threw himself back among the Digger pines and hobbled among the trees like death was at his shoulder, which it almost was. The rifleman hadn't missed him by far, and now the Arrowhead with a visible enemy, was back fighting again, like they always had, to the death.

Dave dodged and ducked until he had partially skirted the ranch yard and saw a clearing ahead of him. There was no choice, and now he knew Roy Murdock, in his present state of mind, would risk everything and anything to kill him without compunction or delay. Murdock had to. Dave Reed was the only living person in the Mesa who could point him out for the things he had done. Murdock's desperate lunge after this final straw that might save him was motivated by the full knowledge that, unless Dave was dead, riddled and blasted without question this time, Arrowhead would be no more.

Murdock shouted at the men. His face was working with a wild, insane passion. "He's in the pines, boys. Two thousand to the one that gets him. Two thousand in gold. Fan out! Don't bunch up there. Fan out and drive him towards an opening."

Dave heard it all and saw the hidden rifleman run up beside Murdock. He swore under his breath. It was the man he had knocked unconscious in back of the blacksmith shed. He was carrying a carbine. Dave raised the appropriated pistol and aligned it easily, but he didn't fire. To do so would expose him to the searching riders. He tried to skirt the opening but had to give it up. There was just one thing to do and he did it. He raced for the trees opposite him as best he could, and heard someone shout behind him, then gunfire rattled and he was across the weed patch and back in the security of the stingy forest and men were yowling after him, closing in fast.

The imminent danger, increasing each second, drove Dave hurriedly before the Arrowhead. He had heard Murdock's offer of two thousand for him, dead. It was an added incentive to forget his bruised and battered body and hunt cover. The thing he needed materialized abruptly, south of the buildings. It was a formidable collection of immense boulders, as tall as a man, apparently tumbled together in this one spot by a giant hand in eons gone. The immediate ground was clear of brush and grass, too, because here Arrowhead cattle came to dust and rub. Thankfully, Dave made it to the rocks, eased in where he had protective, granite covering and waited.

The first Arrowhead man to appear was the pock-faced wispy fellow with the garrulous voice. The man skirted the clearing, bent forward, looking ahead. Dave drew his bead deliberately and squeezed off the shot. The cowboy leaped frenziedly into the air, half-turned and flopped into the brush like a fish out of water. The shot had struck home. Dave smiled to himself. He felt no pity for the man who had so consistently hunted him with killing as his sole objective. Someone yelled farther back. The brush whipped and sawed but Dave couldn't see the riders as they came up, then an ominous, sinister silence set in.

"Reed—you ain't got a chance. We seen you get Shorty. All right, let's see you try an' get out'n them rocks."

The words were punctuated by a rattle of gunfire that made dust fly off the rocks. Reed spat cotton. The sun was starting up, dehydrating the air and he was thirsty and sweating. A small slit afforded frontal sighting. There wasn't any movement, though. He lobbed a rock, waited, and made a wry face. These were no novices. Then a gun exploded off to his left and the slug found a chink in his granite amour and mushroomed not far from his throat. Dave whirled, looked for the man who had discovered the weakness and dumped two straddling shots where he thought the man might be. He was. A rattle of vicious cursing and three fast shots pinned Dave down, then the man, unseen and obviously wounded and raging, screamed his challenge.

"Reed—you son-of-a . . . ! Come out and fight!"

Dave didn't reply. His face twisted coldly and he tossed another slug with sardonic amusement, but the Arrowhead gunman wouldn't be baited. There was a lull Dave used to reload his gun. He felt decidedly uneasy and kept a sharp vigil. Roy Murdock's voice came hollowly out of the trees.

"Reed—you'd better come back out of there."

"Come and get me, Murdock."

"Sure, that's what I'm going to do. I'm coming in without a gun and bring you out a little at a time."

Dave snorted derisively. "You'd better bring the gun, just the same, Murdock. I'm not in a mood to arbitrate, now."

Murdock's scornful laughter floated over the humid compound. "Reed, I wouldn't arbitrate with you if you were the last man on earth. I don't have to."

Dave felt uneasy. He knew Murdock was playing with him and wondered. A furtive appraisal of the little clearing around the rocks showed no Arrowhead men infiltrating. He looked back where Murdock's voice had come from.

"Murdock—Dick Newton and Bar Seven'll be here pretty quick, now. You'd better think it over." It was weak and unconvincing and Dave knew it. He wanted to place that voice for a shot, though. When Murdock answered, though, it was from a different place, nearer, where a finger of buck-brush and wild plum grew inward towards the rocks.

"Let 'em come. When they get here, you won't be around. Not alive, anyway."

"No?" Dave's uneasiness grew instinctively.

"No!" Murdock let it lie there for a moment, then spoke again. "I'll send you a sample of the reason why, Reed."

Dave was puzzled until he saw something round and dully glinting, arch over the brush and land just inside his rock fortress. Understanding came, arm in arm with horror. He made no move to pick the thing up. It wasn't necessary, but the meaning was clear enough. It was a tight, hard rolled stick of dynamite!

Chapter Nine

THE VICTOR

Dave was desperate. He cursed to himself for over-looking Arrowhead's penchant for dynamite. He should have remembered, too, after the way they had blown up his bunkhouse on the meadows.

There were no sounds coming from the brush. Murdock, Dave knew with congealing blood, was fashioning the sticks together that would eradicate him and his stone fortress as well. He raised his six-gun and deliberately fired all six slugs in a calculated pattern of destruction, round the brush thicket where Roy had last called out. The results weren't what he expected at all. Suddenly a twangy voice with a Missouri lilt to it, cried out triumphantly as a burly shouldered man jumped into the clearing brandishing his gun towards Dave's hideout.

"Hold it, Roy. Hold that goddamned bomb. We got him. I counted them shots. He shot her dry that time. Hold her."

The man was loping rapidly across the clearing, firing erratically, recklessly as he charged. Dave was more startled than anything else. He looked at the empty gun, dropped it and fished out the derringer, crouching low. The Arrowhead rider was yelling crazy things to his comrades as he thundered forward. It was a tableau all its own. Even Roy Murdock looked up from where he was fashioning the bomb, listened, then jumped up and pushed forward, where he could watch.

The sounds were close. Dave was thinking fast. The entire episode took less than ten seconds, then he raised up, saw the cowboy's big, black gun raising, thrust the derringer over a rock and fired twice. Each thunderous explosion rolled over the incredulous horrified watchers like a brief paralysis. Dave didn't wait. It was the only chance he'd have, and the poorest he'd ever had, but he grasped it, swung out of the hideout and sprinted past the dead man whose head had been blown apart by the second shot, the only one that touched him, and lying inert and sickening in the thirsty dust.

"Gawd!"

Dave heard it and doubled his speed. The shock wouldn't last. He knew it, but the space to the trees wasn't far either. Luck was with him. The first slug cut branches to his left after he was six feet into the Digger pines and brush. His ankle was telegraphing frantically to his brain that it was going to collapse, which it did as Dave crawled into a mesquite clump, burrowing like a greydigger, regardless of cuts, and lay there, breathing fast and trying to muffle the rasping sounds.

Roy Murdock's voice was a scream of outrage. "Five-thousand, dammit. Five-thousand in gold. Get the . . . Five-thousand and ten broke horses to the man that kills him!"

The gunfire was belt high and probing. Dave heard it and held his breath. He knew Murdock had his bomb made and ready now. Caution seemed to have gripped the Arrowhead men. They were shooting, re-loading and shooting again, raking the hidden places and searching him out with bullets, but they didn't appear to be moving forward so enthusiastically as they had when they'd driven him into the rocks. He lay still, thinking. One slight movement, just a quiver of the brush would bring Murdock's bomb. He pictured the wild, unreasoning look on Roy's face and the way he'd be stalking through the pines searching for the only living witness of his treachery.

The ankle was swollen tight inside his boot-upper. He flicked sweat from his face, saw it was tinted pink with blood from scratches, and ran an exploratory hand over the taut boot-upper. The pain was closer to the surface. It seemed to have been seriously aggravated by the desperate run from the rocks and no longer able to support him. He cursed inwardly and began methodically to reload his six-gun.

The gunfire was desultory and half-hearted, but Dave didn't risk peering out. Not until his breathing was back to normal and the galling silence and inactivity drove him into a kneeling crawl that cleared the sage clump and put him low enough to the ground to see under the shaggy old trees in every direction. There was no movement. He was still lying belly-down, narrow-eyed and cautious, when he heard a familiar sound. It was running horses, many of them, coming fast through the sepulchral vault of the Arrowhead ranch yard, and beyond, sending their dull sounds into the receptive acoustical spaces of the forest fringe. Dave's spirits rose, but he lay still, listening without anything but hope. Then he heard shouting and the gunfire ahead of him stopped abruptly and only the exchange of angry voices floated in, placing the Arrowhead and the posse about six-hundred feet north-west of his hiding place.

Dick Newton's voice was sharp with anxiety. Dave heard the words distinctly enough. "Murdock! Come out'n them woods!" There was no answer and Dave knew Dick was shouting without knowing where Murdock was. He tightened his grip on the six-gun, apprehensively, then Newton's words came out again, through the wilderness. "All right—you there—drop that gun. Come over here." Another voice, low and rumbling, Lester Mallow's, spoke incoherently and Newton answered. "Yeah, good idea, Lester. Take five or six of the boys with you, comb through the brush and kill every one you find that don't drop his guns as soon as you call him."

There was the sound of horses coming ponderously and crashing through the brush and Dave raised himself with the aid of a sapling, stood hanging, and waited. It was Jim Yarbro who saw him first and reined up in amazement.

"Dave! Well—I'll be damned to hell, and that's a fact, boy. You look like you're about seven-eighths dead. Here, give yourself a boost." Yarbro swung down and helped Dave into the saddle, shaking his head in pity. "Damn! No—not that way, Dave. Back over yonder, where the boys are. Lucy's over there, too." Yarbro's voice got insistent and edgy. "Dave—ya damned fool, you're going in the wrong direction. Back over . . ."

"No, Jim. There's a man in here somewhere I want. I'll see you at the yard with the others in a few minutes. Tell Lucy to wait, will you?"

Dave didn't await an answer. It wasn't forthcoming anyway. Jim Yarbro's mouth was hanging open in surprise. He couldn't imagine anyone in Dave Reed's condition even staying in the saddle, let alone speaking coherently.

Dave met Lester as they converged. Neither man spoke. Dave jutted his chin, Indian fashion, towards the Arrowhead yard on their right. Lester followed, allowing his horse to pick its way, looking at Dave from the rear and shaking his head in disbelief. Then they broke into the yard clearing and heard someone off to their right in among the edge of the trees call out.

Dave's gun swung up automatically, but it was Dick Newton spurring wildly towards them, waving his gun-burdened hand as he came. Dave didn't understand the words until Dick was free of the trees. Then he swore and started in the saddle, just in time to see the powerful chestnut roar into the protection of the Mesa Meadows trail, with a hunched-over rider in the saddle. Roy Murdock was escaping!

Jim Yarbro's horse answered the pressure of Dave's knees with a head-jerking lunge that made the rider look down in surprise, then he smiled. He was riding the long-legged, green-broke colt still in the "jaquima". The animal raced recklessly across the yard leaving a wake of dust-devils behind that Lester and Dick squinted against with their eyes as they followed.

The trail was thin but clear. Dave went past the spot where he had downed Jerry Turk in a blurred flash and squinted ahead. Murdock's big chestnut was not far ahead. He couldn't see him, but the dust still hung in the air from his passing. Dave twisted and looked back. Dick and Lester were close together and several hundred yards behind him.

The chase was brief and hectic and Dave emerged into the flat of Mesa Meadows within pistol shot of Roy Murdock. The fleeing rancher twisted and fired. The roar made Dave's colt shy violently but he had anticipated it and was set. He lost precious feet, though, and had to line the colt out again before he could bring him in close enough to Murdock, to shoot. Yarbro's bronc had never been fired off before; he gave a tremendous leap and plunged forward and lit running like the wind, nostrils wide and eyes glassy with fright.

Dave heard Dick and Lester cursing as they fell behind. It was a whisper of anger that was lost in the wild race, then Dave saw the twisted devastation of his log house coming up and raised his pistol, tried to allow his arm a cushioned freedom from the jolting, and fired three times as fast as he could thumb back the hammer. The world came apart in a huge geyser that flung the colt backwards as though it had been struck with a giant paw. Dave and the horse went down in a pinwheel of flying arms and legs and a benevolent blackness closed over both. They were lying where they had fallen when Lester and Dick forced their snorting, wild-eyed horses up beside the downed man and swung to earth.

Dick prised Dave free of the horse and lay his head close to the sweaty, ragged shirt with its tiny thorny-scratch splotches of blood.

Lester's face was chalky. He looked at the crater over

by the bunkhouse wreckage, and back to Dave and touched Dick's arm timidly. "Well?"

"He's alive, Lester. By God, he's alive." The deputy's face swung incredulously towards where Roy Murdock had been. "What—in the name of God—was that?"

Lester passed a shaking hand over his face. "Lord help me, boy, I don't know. Never saw anything like it before in my life. Dave's shots—I heard them. Then—there just wasn't anything but a gawd-awful explosion where Roy and his horse was. Lord! The concussion almost unseated me, as far back as I was. What d'you reckon, Dick? Dynamite?"

"I expect. It had to be something like that. Never heard of a bullet that'd do that." Dick went over to the creek, got a hatful of water and came back and doused Dave's ashen face with it. Strangely, the colt he had been riding stirred first, threshed, grunted, and rolled its eyes. Lester helped the animal up and watched it walk unsteadily and groggily across the meadow, back the way it had come. That was when he saw the other riders coming; Jim Yarbro and Lucy.

Dick fanned Dave's face with the moist hat and watched the color come back slowly, like muddy water, sluggish and reluctant.

The sun was dropping away to the west a little when Dave recognized the perpetual little smile the doctor wore, above him, and spoke.

"The damned fool—still had the bomb, didn't he?"

Dick kneed in closer. "What bomb, Dave?"

Dave sat up listlessly and knuckled his ears. "Hell, it sounds like a waterfall's inside my head."

"I wouldn't be surprised," the doctor said dryly. "The wonder's that you've got a head to hear it in. The concussion just about crushed it flat."

Dick was impatient but gave way when Lucy knelt and put her hand around Dave, drawing him back against her, saying, "Honey, what was it?"

"Murdock . . . He made a dynamite bomb to blast me out of some rocks in that running fight. I'd forgotten all about it when we chased him to the meadows. When I started shooting I had about a tenth of a second when I saw what was happening and remembered the bomb, then I reckon I got caught in the blast." He looked around him at the possemen from Danville, at Jim Yarbro, Lester, Dick and the others and tried a wry smile. "I never thought he'd be totin' the thing with him. Maybe he expected to use it if he could maneuver all of us into one spot long enough to toss it."

Dick looked pointedly at the wrecked bunkhouse. "He was dynamite happy, the idiot."

Lucy bent a little and kissed Dave's forehead and the fragrance of her was relaxing in his nostrils. He looked up at the others, saw their drawn, harassed looks, and waved a hand at them.

"How about if we ride to Bar Seven after a buggy. You look pretty used up for saddle-back riding." Lester wasn't looking at the deputy when he shook his head in agreement.

Lucy was blushing when Dick looked at her. Understanding didn't come fully until Jim Yarbro's boot-toe surreptitiously gigged Newton's leg, then he got up with jerky, fast movements and made a self-conscious face.

"Well—of course. What was I thinking of, anyway?"

They mounted slowly, looking significantly at one another, and the doctor spoke dryly to no one in particular.

"He's half sly, at that, boys. The man's got a badly sprained ankle, among other assorted wounds and lacerations." He reined after the others wagging his head back and forth. "I still don't think he knows just how tough he is."

Lester was the last over the lip of the undulating plain that was Mesa Meadows. He didn't look back sneakily. This was his only daughter and she was locked in the embrace of the man Lester Mallow had long schemed to jar out of his reckless inertia long enough to make him a first class cowman. He saw them kiss. He sighed, reined back and followed Newton who was waiting for him, and for the first time in many years, Lester Mallow was whistling a lilting song of a cowboy's love.

Center Point Publishing
600 Brooks Road • PO Box 1
Thorndike ME 04986-0001 USA

(207) 568-3717

US & Canada:
1 800 929-9108